Deadly Cellmate

Longarm lay on the cement floor of a dinky prison cell, dimly lit by one dinky window, which was covered with a rusty grill and too high to gaze out of. The door was solid oak, crisscrossed with riveted iron straps.

Making a deal with T. J. Perkins would be a lot like signing a pact with the Devil, except for the fact that the Prince of Darkness was said to be a fiend of his word. Perkins was an international jewel thief who'd gotten the drop on two U.S. Customs agents and executed them in cold blood.

Longarm reached for a smoke, recalled with a curse that he didn't even have a burnt-out match stem, and said, "I'd trust a rascal like you about as far as I'd trust the rurale who hit me on the head just now. But I fail to see how anyone born half as honest as me could hope to break out of this solid-looking box."

"Do you think we might make it?" asked T.J. with renewed interest.

"No. But I'd rather get shot than strangled, wouldn't you?"

Also in the LONGARM series
from Jove

TABOR EVANS

LONGARM

AND THE DAY OF DEATH

JOVE BOOKS, NEW YORK

LONGARM AND THE DAY OF DEATH

A Jove Book / published by arrangement with
the author

PRINTING HISTORY
Jove edition / August 1989

ISBN: 0-515-10107-9

PRINTED IN THE UNITED STATES OF AMERICA

10 9 8 7 6 5 4 3 2 1

Chapter 1

Longarm wasn't looking for a fight when he strode into the Nuevo Laredo lockup. But fighting Longarm just seemed to come natural to Mexican lawmen, so he'd no sooner shown the desk sergeant his I.D. and the extradition papers he'd come packing so peaceably when he wound up on the floor with eight or ten sweaty rurales on top of him.

One of them had grabbed Longarm's six-gun from its cross-draw holster under his tweed frock coat as they were all going down together. He still might have managed to get at the derringer in his vest pocket had not the same son of a bitch smacked him atop the skull with his own gun and knocked him silly for a spell.

He got to jellyfish in a sea of ink for some unfathomable eons, then he finally noticed a sort of ruby glow that seemed to be coming through his eyelids. So he opened them. But things didn't look a speck more cheerful.

He lay on the cement floor of a dinky prison cell, dimly lit by one dinky window, which was covered with a rusty grill and too high to gaze out of. The door was solid oak, crisscrossed with riveted iron straps. There was nothing in the way of furnishings. Another prisoner sat in one corner with his back to the rough stucco. He wore nothing but his pants and shirt, and both looked as gringo as the face of the middle-aged man wearing them. So Longarm propped himself up on one elbow, noting that he seemed to be barefoot in just his pants and hickory shirt as well, and said, "Howdy. If you'd be T. J. Perkins, I have orders to transport you back to the federal district court. I had 'em when I crossed the border, leastways. The sons of bitches didn't even leave me with lint in my pockets."

The older man nodded soberly and said, "Los rurales are like that. You'll never know how much I was looking forward to going back to the states as your prisoner. For even if I can't convince a yanqui judge and jury of my innocence, I'd still rather hang on or above my native soil than go the way we'll both be going when these greasers get around to it. They told me they meant to save a lot of bother by having gringos just sort of vanish, once you got here. They said Tio Sam was loco en la cabeza to be sending the one and original Longarm here to pick me up. How come you're so popular with los rurales, Deputy Long?"

Longarm rubbed the top of his aching head with his free hand as he explained, "This particular rurale post must not have kept abreast of the times. It's true I've enjoyed a few artillery exchanges with Mexico in the past. I mentioned that when my boss, Marshal Bill Vail, said he wanted me to come down here and pick you up because you were so unusually murderous, T.J. But, you see, I saved the lives of some rurales in El Paso not long ago and we thought I'd been forgiven. We're all supposed to be lawmen, after all. How come they want to be so mean to you? Seems to me the reward on you in the states has to be

2

worth more than the boots and hat they stole from you."

The wanted killer sighed and said, "I pointed that out to them. They said it was my misfortune and none of their own that bounty papers on me specify dead or alive. After we've both been dead a spell they meant to discover me dead and never discover you at all. I think we'd better forget about the past and see if we can work something out together, as fellow Americans in distress, don't you?"

Longarm didn't answer until he'd hauled himself into another corner to sit up with his back to the wall and his bare heels planted on the only slightly smoother cement floor. He knew it was time he made a deal with *some*-damned-body. But making one with old T. J. Perkins would be a lot like signing a pact with the Devil, except for the fact that the Prince of Darkness was said to be a fiend of his word.

Perkins was an international jewel thief and diamond smuggler, which was bad enough, who'd gotten the drop on two U.S. Customs agents and executed them in cold blood, which was worse. It was Longarm's understanding that his fellow prisoner had given his word he'd come quiet if only they'd allow him to kiss his innocent sweetheart adios. She was the one who'd likely passed him the gun after the two dumb federal agents had searched him and got to acting stupid. Longarm reached absently for a smoke, recalled with a curse that he didn't even have a burnt-out match stem, and said, "I'd trust a rascal like you about as far as I'd trust the rurale who hit me on the head just now. But I'm listening. For I fail to see how anyone born half as

3

honest as me could hope to bust out of this solid-looking box."

The older and less honest man in the other corner said, "They know they have us at their mercy. And los rurales don't have much in the way of mercy. We might be able to appeal to their sense of greed."

Longarm nodded and said, "Far be it from me to say they don't seem greedy bastards. But what might we have, between us, to greed anybody with? They never even left us our socks."

"They know you were sent to pick up a famous, ah, diamond broker," Perkins said. "What if you were to confide to them, behind my back, of course, that you suspected I'd stashed a king's ransom in uncut and untraceable stones before they picked me up in that house of ill repute the other night? They know I had nothing like that on me. They'll have searched the cathouse high and low by now. I've told 'em, more than once, I was between engagements and almost broke when they picked me up. I don't like to get beat up any more than the next man. I'm sure I had 'em convinced, 'till you showed up just now. But if you were to say you'd been told I was laying low in Mexico with a fortune in diamonds—"

"It won't work," Longarm cut in. "I've tried to make deals with rurales before. That's how come I managed to be on such swell terms with more than one in the past. We might keep ourselves alive a day or more longer by leading them on a snipe hunt. But they ain't about to let us out of their sight for one whole second, and we'd just wind up getting treated Apache in the end. I'd just as soon get killed slow and sloppy without added trimmings, if it's all the same to you. With luck, they might just shoot us.

4

Mex hangmen have a lot to learn, and an old boy can dangle a spell staring up a rope with his toes just off the dust. They seem to find the dancing comical. They're mean to bulls as well. Must have something to do with all the praying they get put through when they're little."

Old T.J. insisted, "I've never seen why they make such a fuss out of knifing a cow, either, and damn it, we're only a hop, skip, and jump from Texas!"

Longarm shrugged and said, "There's a river to cross and, next to sticking bulls, there's nothing they enjoy more than shooting at a running target knee-deep in quicksand. Los rurales are issued U.S. Cavalry model Colt .45's and, while I hate to say it, most of the bastards are good shots. Try harder. Getting out of this cell is the least of our worries. It's staying alive within a quarter mile of yonder door we got to worry about."

T.J. pouted, "We can't make even a dumb move while we're still in here. I've heard you can move fast as spit on a hot stove, in spite of your size, and I've been known to move sudden when the occasion calls for it."

Longarm smiled thinly and said, "So my boss told me when he ordered me to use leg irons as well as handcuffs to carry you home. Just for the record, we never got the name of that gal you knew so well. Neither customs agent thought to write down her name as you left 'em dying in New Orleans that time."

The older man chuckled fondly and said, "I never kiss and tell. I'd sure like to get my hands on a false-hearted woman here in Nuevo Laredo, though. It just ain't decent to screw a man for money and then turn him over to the law. Never trust a puta with a rose in her hair, Longarm."

"I have learned to my sorrow not to trust more than one gringa with blue eyes and an innocent smile. But boasting of our love lives ain't about to get us out of this fix. Would you say these walls are plastered-over field stone or just thick adobe?"

T.J. shrugged and said, "Feel free to start gnawing with your teeth. If they ever get around to feeding us again you'll find the soup du jour is lots of pepper and water with a little tripe, and that it's served in clay bowls without any spoons. If they left us a spoon, or, hell, a table knife, it would take more than one night to dig through even 'dobe. I'm sort of surprised they haven't come for us already, now that they have you in here with me."

Longarm decided, "They must not be planning on a public rope dance. Let's see, I got jumped before I'd had the chance to eat lunch. How long was I out?"

T.J. shrugged and said, "An hour or so. You sure do cuss in your sleep. What difference does that make?"

"It's still early afternoon," Longarm said. "Likely siesta time. If that ain't it, they're planning on doing us in after dark. I hope they don't cuff us as they lead us out. I can't run half as fast with my hands behind my back."

"Do you think we might make it?" asked T.J. with renewed interest.

"No. But any chance has to be better than no chance at all, and I'd rather get shot than strangled, wouldn't you?"

The older man looked as if he was fixing to cry.

6

Longarm said, "No shit, about that gal in New Orleans . . ."

But T.J. grimaced and told Longarm to just go to Hell, adding, "With my luck you'd be the one to get away and— Oh, sure, I see what you and your rurale pals are up to, now. This whole thing was cooked up by you sneaky lawmen just to see if you could get me to peach on that sweet little thing! You can ask your pals to let you out now. It ain't going to work and I'd just as soon we caught that train now. You know you got to feed me three meals a day while I'm in U.S. federal custody."

Longarm didn't answer. He could see how such a suspicious natured crook had lasted long enough to go a mite gray around the edges. He'd learned to consider everyone he met along the owlhoot trail as low down and double dealing as himself. Wasn't he in for a surprise when the two of 'em wound up dead together!

But while Longarm was far from disappointed, later that same day things worked out less predictably. They came for old T.J. first. When Longarm got up to go with them one of the rurales who'd come for the older man shoved Longarm back against the wall and said, "Not you, *Brazo Largo*. Maybe we can talk about the Alamo, later. *We* have been taught to remember the Alamo, too!"

Longarm replied, "That seems fair. Only I wasn't born yet, and if I had been, it still wouldn't have been in Texas. I'm a West-by-God-Virginia boy myself, and the only serious war I ever rode in was between the Blue and the Gray. I kinda forget which side I was on in my misspent youth, but I can't recall many Mexican gents fighting for either, so . . ."

7

Then they were gone and it wasn't much fun to pace a cell in bare feet. He paced some, anyway. A million years went by and then, as the sunset outside was painting orange checks and purple shadows on the stucco and he was really starting to get hungry, the door popped open again to let his boots, hat, and frock coat fly in at him. As they landed, the rurale who'd tossed them to the floor growled, "Get dressed. You seem to have friends in high places. My sainted mother always warned me this was an unjust world."

Longarm didn't argue. He even found his socks in a pocket of his otherwise deserted frock coat. His vest had been stuffed down one boot. He just got dressed as fast as he could manage, seated on cement. Then the rurale led him out to the front office. They'd tidied it up since he'd tried so hard to wreck it. The desk sergeant handed over his gun rig, .44-40 six-gun and all, along with a fat manila envelope containing his personal belongings, save some cash he'd had in his wallet along with his badge and I.D. He didn't comment on this. He just put the loose change they'd left him in his duds, along with his pocketknife, waterproof matches, three-for-a-nickel cheroots and such. The desk sergeant pointed with undisguised disgust at an expensively suited Mex with patent-leather hair and told Longarm to go someplace else with his lawyer before they changed their minds. So he did.

Outside, in the jasmine-scented air of a Mexican evening, Longarm turned to the total stranger and said, "You'll never know how glad I am to meet you, even if we've never met before. Who sent you, the American Consulate?"

8

The dapper Mex put his rakish Panama hat back on to take Longarm's arm as he replied, "My clients are Americano, pero not connected with your own government, as far as I know. I am called Gomez. *Señor* Gomez if you do not mind. I did not, how you say, bail you out because I adore your big gray eyes and heroic mustachio. My mother's elder brother died at El Alamo, on *our* side. I am taking you, now, to the people who retained my services as the best *abogado* in Nuevo Laredo, if not all Estada Chihuahua. They can tell you why they wished you out of La Carcel. With all due respect, I do not care."

Longarm agreed that sounded fair and, as they headed for more fashionable parts of the border town, asked Gomez if he had any notion as to what might have happened to the other gringo he'd come all this way to pick up in the first place. The lawyer just shrugged and said they might tell him where he was going, if they wanted to.

When they got there in the gathering dusk, Gomez led him in through a sweet-smelling patio to the candle-lit main room of the house. There they found a pretty gal wearing light brown hair and a low-cut French-blue dress that almost matched her eyes. That is to say, Longarm found her. The lawyer who'd brought him seemed to have vanished in a puff of distaste for both their kind. She patted the leather sofa she was seated on near a baronial but cold fireplace, saying, "Please be good enough to join me, Deputy Long. We have a lot to talk about."

He removed his hat and sat down beside her, agreeing they sure must have, adding, "Might you have been the one as bailed T. J. Perkins out, earlier, ma'am?"

She dimpled at him and said without a trace of guilt in her throaty contralto, "Of course. Los rurales never let *anyone* out without being paid off. I thought it best to get that shabby old criminal out well ahead of you, give him some money along with railroad tickets, and let him get a good lead on you. My name is Patricia O'Boyne, by the way. My friends call me Paddy. I own and operate the O Bar B spread up near the headwaters of the Pecos. Or I do when nobody's trying to steal my late father's land grant, at any rate."

Longarm nodded and said, "Raising beef along the Pecos sounds wholesome, Miss Paddy. Turning wanted killers loose don't. Is this some sort of game we're supposed to be playing? You don't *look* loco en la cabeza. But, no offense, I just can't fathom why anyone would want to give a killer a good lead on the law and then say right out which way he went."

She picked up a bitty brass bell from the nearby coffee table, dinged it, and put it back down as she replied, "I don't care one way or the other about that nasty old outlaw. I want you to head for Mexico City with me. I need an armed escort and they say you know how to fight with your fists as well, if you have to."

Longarm stared at her, thundergasted, as a pretty mestiza maid came in to answer that jingle with a silver tray of goodies. As she placed the tray before them on the table and crawfished back to the kitchen, Longarm resisted the hungry impulse to grab one of those swell-looking tacos, saying, instead, "I thank you for the handsome compliment, Miss Paddy, and that coffee smells grand as well. But where did you get the notion I work as an armed escort for even a lady pretty as yourself? I'm a paid-up rider for the U.S. Department of Justice. I'm here, barely inside of Mexico, to pick up one T. J. Perkins and carry him back. That's all either Mex or U.S. law allows me to do."

She nodded and began to pour for them both as she said calmly, "That's why I gave the man you came for a head start on you. Once we get to the capital you'll be free to look for him and do anything you like to him. I have friends in high places there as well. I'm sure they'll be willing to help you look him up again."

Seeing she was still offering, Longarm picked up a taco, bit at least a third of it off, and washed down the results with her swell coffee, taking it black, before he asked with dawning interest why she just couldn't hire some tough Mex if she felt all that nervous about riding a train alone. He added, "El Presidente Diaz frowns on having first-class passengers robbed on his personal railroads, even when they're light complected, Miss Paddy."

She smiled wearily and said, "Heavens, I'm not worried about getting along with most Mexicans, Deputy Long. I'm fluent in the language and respectful of the customs down here. The enemies I'm worried about may or may not be Americano. Perhaps I'd better begin at the beginning?"

He swallowed the last of that first taco, reached for another, and said, "I sure wish you would. Nothing you've said so far makes much sense. But you can call me Custis, anyway, Miss Paddy."

She said she would and began, "Once upon a time when the old Spanish Empire was still in business,

11

an Irish wild goose, in the service of His Most Catholic Majesty, was retired to the new world with a royal grant to quite a bit of the upper Pecos Valley. In those days Spain owned most everything west of the Lousiana Purchase, you see."

Longarm nodded and said, "I know about Spanish land grants. I read more than some figure I might, despite appearance. When Mexico busted free of Spain back in twenty-one it honored the terms of the old royal grants, a heap of Mex leaders having been granted the same. When we licked Mexico fair and square in the late forties, one of the conditions of the peace treaty was that Mexican citizens stuck on all that land we'd taken from Mexico would have the same rights as U.S. nationals, since that was what they had to be now, whether they wanted to be or not. Washington agreed to honor the property deeds granted to Spanish or Mex settlers by their previous governments. I doubt anyone back East knew how *much* land the old Spanish kings might have granted most anyone for modest favors, but there was even more left over and so there we all was."

He washed down some more taco before he added, "I don't see what you have to worry about if you own one of them old Spanish grants, Miss Paddy. Some would-be land grabbers have tried to contest such deeds in the years since Uncle Sam agreed to honor 'em in full. The Irvine Grant out California way is so big that the present-day descendents of a Scotch sea captain and a pretty señorita still get lost on it. The state of California, now that it's run by English-talking political hacks, has tried more than once to say it just ain't right for one family to own so much land between San Diego and Pueblo de Los Angeles. You can't hardly get from one to the other without riding over Irvine land. But the federal courts have backed the now much paler family every time it's come up."

She shushed him with a sigh and said, "It's not that simple in my case. My great grandfather's original grant, signed by the king of Spain, is on file at the federal building in Santa Fe. My problem is that a land grabber, as you'd call him, has come forth to claim the original grant was a forgery, and that the old records of the Spanish viceroy in Ciudad Mejico fail to back our claim up. They naturally kept copies of every such land grant, you see."

Longarm nodded and replied, "They make me put stuff down in triplicate and hardly any of it's that important. But what's all the fuss about, Miss Paddy? Can't you just get a lawyer like old Gomez to look things up in Mexico City and prove that other cow baron a big fibber?"

"That was the first thing I thought of. I naturally wired a prominent law firm down there to see if they could check the old records out for me. They did. Alas, it seems my great grandfather was a bit of a rogue. There *is* such a grant in the old Spanish viceroy's records, but made out to a Spanish family whose main line has been extinct for some time. I don't know what ever possessed my rival ranchero to even think of looking up now-poor and distant relatives of the original grant holder. But he did, and bought their land rights from *them*, for next to nothing. The poor dears couldn't have known what they were signing away. I'd have given them a much better deal."

Longarm whistled softly and said, "So would I, if

13

I found out my family had been squatting all this time on someone else's land. Whatever happened to the Spanish grantee the king of Spain was *really* fonder of, Miss Paddy?"

"Nobody knows, after all this time. I'd like to think it was Indians or the pox. A lot of folk died of either in the early days of Nuevo Mejico. But whether my great grandfather was really evil or simply a forger, I still consider the O Bar B family property, damn it! My father and his father before him were born on our old grant, as I was, no matter how it might have come into the family. It's just mean as anything for another outfit to steal my old homestead and all that range from me just by giving a dirt-poor Mex some drinking money!"

Longarm hauled out a smoke, held it up for her to nod yes or no, and when she nodded, he lit it and got it going before he told her gently, "That's the way things work out, sometimes, Miss Paddy. You should hear some Lakota carry on about the Black Hills. I thought they got skinned, too. But, then, if I knew how to think like a lawyer I might like the species better. I'd sure like to help you out, if I had any notion how I might, but . . ."

"Just get me to the hall of records in Ciudad Mejico alive and well. There's only one conflicting claim in one old musty ledger."

He frowned and said, "Hold on. I can't say I admire the Diaz government they got down here right now. But asking me to help you crook even a dead viceroy's records about land *inside* the present borders of the U.S. of A. is asking way too much of a man who packs a badge of the same!"

14

She insisted, "I'm not asking you to do anything illegal."

"You just want me to get you there so *you* can crook 'em, right?"

She shook her head and told him, "I might not have to. How do we know someone didn't switch the records to begin with? My Mexican law firm reported that the old ledgers are falling apart, with a lot of the pages loose. Each grant of land or patent of nobility consists of one big sheet of parchment, signed and sealed by long-dead officials and bound together in leather-bound ledgers the years and dry air of the capital have not been kind to, so—"

"So *we*," Longarm cut in, "mean to sort of slip out the rival claim and slip in our own copy of your great granddad's royal grant, suitably antiqued with a good soak in say, strong tea, followed by a good long sunbath, right?"

She met his gaze with an unflinching smile as she sort of purred, "My what a clever man you are. I never would have thought of that."

He smiled thinly and replied, "I wouldn't have thought of it myself if I had not arrested some forgers in my time. Tea stains old treasure maps and such just right, while there's nothing like a few days worth of bright New Mexico sunlight to fade ink the way it might get old, more natural, on a bookshelf. Do you want to show me the sheet of brittle parchment you mean to make your switch with? I can't arrest you here in Mexico and I'd be prouder to give you some tips than I might be to ride all the way down to Mexico City with you."

She lowered her lashes and murmured, "Alas, I don't have such a document. Whether you believe me or not, you still have to go south if you mean to recapture that killer they sent you after."

He nodded and said, "Thanks to you, I reckon I do. But I've found it to be true that he travels faster who travels alone and, no offense, Miss Paddy, you make me sort of tense. I can't say for certain whether it's that perfume you got on or that talk about you having enemies you need to be guarded against. How come you think you need your *body* guarded if the fuss is over *land* clean over to New Mexico? If half of what you just said is true, that rascal disputing your land grant has got you. Why should he risk harming a hair on your head when he's got such a swell chance of beating you in court?"

She looked as if she was trying not to cry as she told him, "That was the way it looked to me when I slipped south from San Miguel County a few nights ago. Our family lawyer said he could delay the case a few months with luck and a present for the judge, but that sooner or later I was sure to lose my land unless I could prove the other side's charges false. I meant to streak directly south, of course. But when I got to El Paso I noticed I was being followed. So I pretended to board the southbound at Juarez, slipped off the other side, and caught the eastbound for Laredo instead."

"Do you suspect you were followed here?" he asked.

"I don't know. This house belongs to old and trusted business associates of my late father. I was only planning to stay here a day or so and make a run for it once I felt sure it was safe. When I heard both you and the killer you'd come for had been grabbed by los rurales I had a better idea. I told you about *that*."

He nodded and said, "You sure have and I have to say it's been mighty interesting. But I got me a train to catch right now. So if it's all the same to you—"

"You can't," she cut in. "The last train for Ciudad Mejico left some time ago, with that Perkins creature aboard it. I made sure it was the last train, tonight, before I had Gomez set you free. The next train south leaves tomorrow morning. We'll both be aboard it whether you like it or not and, if you'll only be a little reasonable, you can ride all the way in the comfort of the private compartment I've booked, at no cost to you or the U.S. taxpayers."

He laughed despite himself and said, "You really do deserve a good spanking. But I've ridden third class on a Mex train before and it is a long day's trip, Lord willing and the banditos don't tear up the track. So I'll sleep on your invite. Meanwhile I'd best find me some safe place to sleep."

"What's the matter with here? The folk who own this place are away right now, as you may have noticed. So we have it all to ourselves tonight."

He started to tell her not to talk silly. Then he wondered why anyone would want to say a silly thing like that. He leaned back and said, "Well, if you have a guest room..." But when they got tired of talking, around midnight, that wasn't where he wound up.

Chapter 2

It would have been rude to turn down a first-class railroad ride from a lady he'd ridden first-class half the night. It would have been sort of dumb as well. For like everything else run by the Diaz dictatorship, there was no such thing as middle-class on the national railroads of Mexico these days. Peones got to sit on wooden benches or the floor with pigs and chickens, while the high-toned folk got to ride better than they might have in the states. The private compartment Paddy had booked came with its own running water and fancy Edison lights. For the varnished car was fresh from the Pullman plant near Chicago.

Longarm had barely stowed their baggage and hung up his hat and coat before the train started smack on time, the way trains were supposed to in a dictatorship, on pain of death. It was early morn, of course, so Longarm pulled down the curtains when Paddy proceeded to get undressed for bed without even asking if he wanted more slap and tickle.

Once she'd spread her naked charms on the fold-down bunk, however, he didn't really feel the need of a formal invitation to join her atop the starched linen. He knew it figured to get too hot before it got too cool for daylight lovemaking, and while he'd thought he'd seen all she had to offer by candlelight the night before, she looked even better in the all-to-

18

gether by the bright green glow coming through the shades.

He made sure the door was locked, hung his gun rig handy by the head of the bunk, and wedged his derringer between the pillows and mahogany bulkhead before he started to shuck himself.

By the time he was down to his socks she was writhing about and begging him to dammit hurry. So he rolled aboard her, socks and all, like one of those rascals on a French postcard. From the way they posed, those sassy French gals likely wanted to get right down to business, too. He and Paddy hadn't gotten down to all the sassy stuff in the darkness of that bedroom the night before. She'd wasted too much time on the usual protestations that she wasn't that kind of a girl before she'd proven to him she was and, by that time, they'd had to consider getting at least some sleep lest they miss the train.

But now that they were on it and didn't even have to change at Monterrey, she seemed to want to try everything that didn't hurt. He was willing. It surely had the scenery outside beat as she presented him with some mighty interesting views of her anatomy. She'd told him she'd grown up on a cattle spread and, while she was built curvaceous as any man would desire a woman to be built, there wasn't an ounce of flab on her athletic young body. Even her pert breasts were solid as a pair of big ripe peaches. She said she admired his horseman's hips as he posted in her love saddle, once they got down to cases and quit fooling around so French. But in the end it seemed she might have bitten off more than she'd really been up to chewing, at both ends. For he'd only brought her to climax thrice before she just

19

closed her eyes and commenced to snore, refined, with a satisfied little smile on her lips.

They hadn't been riding more than an hour or so, and Longarm was always wide awake at this hour in any case. So he gently rolled off her, lit a cheroot, and slid the curtain up enough to stare out at Mexico some more. On this line south they were east of the high tablelands Mexico City and a heap of cactus perched on. So the scenery was more dry subtropical than high desert. Spanish bayonet and half-ass little palm trees rose above high chaparral between towns. The bitty pueblos they whipped through without stopping were partly shaded by feathery pepper trees and plantana, which was a sort of tasteless banana Mexicans admired because it grew farther north than sweet bananas and wasn't bad, fried like potatoes.

The humble ill-served settlements of common folk betrayed the holes of El Presidente's grandiose plans for a modern Mexico, and explained all the rebel bands infesting the place to everyone but the assholes running it.

General Porfirio Diaz, who'd fought well for Juarez, to give a devil his due, had elected himself when the sincerely patriotic Benito Juarez had died back in '76. Less educated than the pure Indian Juarez, the part-white Diaz had turned out more ambitious and less patient. Juarez had been forced to fight to get Mexico back from outsiders after earlier governments had put the whole country in hock to foreign investors. Diaz had gone right back to running the country in the red and, for the upper classes, he *was* doing a fair job at catching up with the Jones boys. This very railroad, built and stocked by investors in London or on Wall Street, was a worthy rival to the

Union Pacific or Santa Fe. It charged less for first-class passage and moved the freight of grantees who were in with Diaz at a loss. Since *somebody* had to pay off the foreign stockholders, little folk who didn't know anybody important got to pay through the nose for piss-poor service. Taxes were collected the same way. Big rancheros paid next to nothing per acre because, to Diaz, a hacienda was a hacienda and you paid as much land tax on a bitty one-family farm as you might a ranch bigger than, say, Maryland. Los rurales and, if that didn't work, the federal army, saw that everyone paid what Diaz considered his fair share of taxes. So naturally they had to be paid and equipped about as well as the U.S. Army and, if they needed more, felt free to just take it, as long as they didn't mess with anyone Diaz admired. He didn't seem to think much of common Mex folk, and was prone to call them greasers in the company of his rich pals from El Norte.

A deserted little water mill they whipped past reminded Longarm of some other bitches he'd heard from Mex friends about the new prosperity of Mexico. It was purely true that the dictator had done much to modernize industry down here. Factories, run as well as financed by outsiders, had sprung up like weeds since Diaz had taken over. They even provided employment for those Mexicans educated enough to run mysterious machinery imported from other parts of the world. So far, Diaz hadn't built school-one to educate anyone *else*. In a country that was ninety percent illiterate as well as barefoot, mass production served to make the chronic unemployment worse, as it put the cottage industries of a farming and ranching society out of business. Before Diaz, just about every village had needed its own grist mill, pottery, one-man cabinet shop and such. Even a family without its own corn patch had been able to get by spinning and weaving by hand. Longarm had long admired the clever handcrafts of a patient and not unskilled people. Now, save fancy work for the tourist trade, the old village artisans just couldn't compete with the factory products churned out so cheap. The new factories didn't sell stuff cheap because Diaz felt all that generous. Mexico just didn't need much cotton cloth, tinware, leather goods and such. So the few rich kept getting richer and the poor majority just kept getting more miserable. Diaz was only about fifty right now, seemed to be in good health for a gent who lived so high on the hog, and thus a heap of Mexicans felt they just couldn't wait until he died natural. And so, instead of sharing with even half the little folk, Diaz was inclined to have 'em die younger than he figured on dying. It was a hell of a way to run a country, even if the railroads did run on time down here.

By the time he'd smoked down his cheroot Longarm was finding the scenery tedious, and when he snubbed out the smoke and kissed one of Paddy's pert nipples she just moaned and rolled over with her bare back to him. He rolled off the bunk and washed off at the handy water tap, swishing his teeth fresh while he was at it. The gal was still snoring sweet as ever. So he sat on the mahogany seat of the commode between the bunk and locked door to see if she had anything interesting to read in the one leather grip he'd carried aboard for her along with his carpetbag of possibles. He found what he suspected he might in a pasteboard mailing tube. The spidery script was in Spanish so old-time he could barely read it. Whoever she'd gotten to grant all that New Mexico range to her great grandfather in the name of the king of Spain had sure aged hell out of the sheepskin with something brown, and he thought the frayed silk ribbons stuck to the forgery with old remelted sealing wax was a nice touch. He rolled it up and stuck it back in its tube, lest she awake to find a gent who'd just loved her had been right about what she was planning to pull off. As he snapped her grip shut she stirred in her sleep to ask what was going on. He slid her grip back where he'd found it and rejoined her atop the sheeting to ask if she wanted to get kissed some more. She sighed that she was dammit asleep. So he let go of her, lit another smoke, and just lay there pondering the perfidity of womankind.

It wasn't as if he had to help her sneak into the hall of records once they got there. To begin with he didn't know where the place was, and in any case he had no jurisdiction. He'd begin by arresting one Porfirio Diaz if he had. He felt sure that even a dictatorship had to have some laws covering forgery. But they were up to Mex lawmen to enforce and he didn't really like to think of anyone so pretty being questioned by the current Mex lawmen. He blew a thoughtful smoke ring as he considered the laws of New Mexico Territory. Since New Mexico wasn't a state, it was run by a federally appointed governor, with the various incorporated counties running things to suit their local selves. So her planned shell game with another resident of San Miguel County could read local jurisdiction, if you didn't squint too close, and Longarm was a live-and-let-live cuss with enough on his plate. It only stood to reason that a cow baron out to screw such a great lay out of the spread she'd been born on had the duty to look out for his own damned interests and, if his fancy lawyers were dumb enough to let the little lady get away with a ruse so obvious, the cuss didn't deserve the range in dispute.

That left him nothing to do but stare out at the passing scenery some more. He found it a mite more interesting now that some cusses wearing big straw sombreros and crisscrossed ammo belts seemed to be loping along out there, waving horse pistols at the train. He reached absently for his handy .44-40 just as one of the rebels, bandits or whatever fired a shot that made the outside wall of their compartment shudder some. Longarm cranked open the window and fired a shot across the bows of the noisy cuss, hoping to make him reconsider before someone got hurt.

Paddy, between him and the window sill, awoke with a start to ask, or rather scream, "What happened? Was that a shot?"

He shoved her back down and said, "Yep. Train seems to be under attack. Keep your pretty head down lest they see what a swell prize they could be riding off with."

The rider in the lead fired again and would have showered both their naked bodies with busted glass if he hadn't aimed high enough to mostly punch a hole through the canvas curtain. Longarm muttered, "Well, I tried to warn you, damn it . . ." This time he took aim before he replied in kind to such rudeness. He emptied the leader's saddle and then, when they still kept cussing and shooting back, emptied two

24

more to see if he could convince them of the error of their ways.

He must have. They all reined in and whipped back out of his sight, even though he still heard other guns going off like bitty firecrackers somewhere to the rear. He swung his bare feet to the floor and told Paddy, "Slip something on, sudden. The train crew is surely going to want to know if everyone aboard is still with 'em."

They did. But by the time they were pounding on the door, Longarm was decently dressed, and a lady had every right to wrap herself in a kimono in her own private compartment.

As Longarm slid the door open he was expecting to talk to just a porter or conductor. He was glad he'd holstered his gun when he saw the federale major standing there with the conductor. The cuss looked excited as well as armed and dangerous. Longarm greeted them in Spanish to say he'd noticed, but that save some busted glass he had no damage to report. The major told him he was too modest, ripped one of the medals off his uniform—he had plenty to spare —and pinned it to Longarm's shirt before he kissed him on both cheeks like a French general, saying, "You got El Sombrero Blanco. He landed on his head and two of his men rode over him for to knock the rest of his thrice-accursed soul out of him. That was lovely shooting, yanqui! How are you called, in order that I may put your nombre in my official report about the death of El Sombrero Blanco?"

Longarm muttered, "Aw, mush, I wasn't the only one shooting back at the rascals, Major. Why don't you just put down that you got him yourself and save us all the bother with the newspaper reporters? That *is* a U.S. Army sharpshooter's medal under the fancier one with the gold eagle, isn't it?"

The Mex major replied modestly, "I was trained at West Point, of course. But I am sure you were the one who spilled the leader just now. He fell just as I was about to fire."

"I'm sure you must have hit him on the way down," Longarm said. "I'd just hate to rob a federale officer of his due, me being a stranger in your country and all."

So after some consideration they shook on it. Longarm gave the medal back, and was free to slide the door shut again and turn back to Paddy, saying, "I just hate it when they try to rob a train I'm trying to ride incognito. Don't you?"

She laughed like hell and invited him back to bed, opening her kimono by way of added inspiration. He said, "Hold the thought. We'll be stopping to jerk water at Monterrey any minute, and what just happened is sure to cause some excitement. I'd hate to have them trying to fix that window while we were going at it, come to study on it."

So they were both seated sedate with the bunk folded back up when their train stopped at Monterrey, and he'd been right about the efficient ways of the national railroad. He watched with mild interest and some admiration as the yard workers made short work of the window putty and slapped new panes back in place as if they were used to doing such chores a lot. Knowing the whole north of Mexico was aboil with unemployed farm boys turned outlaw, it was safe to assume they did.

The sky the Mex workmen were outlined against

26

was gray and gloomy, despite all the sunshine they'd just passed through. The once sleepy city of Monterrey had changed considerably since the days Mexico and the U.S. Army had fought over it.

Longarm had been too young to run off to that particular war, even as a drummer boy, but he'd seen the Currier and Ives prints, and they assured one and all that the autumn skies above the then-white walls of the old Spanish town had been a bright cloudless blue as the doomed captives from the San Patricio Brigade had watched and waited from a nearby hilltop for the victory that would mean their mass death.

The San Patricios were Irish Catholics, a lot of them deserters from the U.S. Army, who'd chosen to fight on the Mexican side. A platoon or more of 'em had been taken alive in the battle for Monterrey, so Zach Taylor had ordered that they be allowed to live long enough to see the Stars and Stripes rise over the Bishop's palace in the center of town as they enjoyed a last smoke with ropes around their necks. It sounded sort of chickenshit to Longarm. The San Patricios couldn't have admired old Zach Taylor all that much as the Stars and Stripes went up and they all went down to the ends of those ropes together. But, at any rate, the skies of Monterrey weren't blue these days. There was coal and iron ore in the surrounding hills. So Monterrey had been turned into Mexico's answer to Pittsburgh, with smelters spewing smoke and soot around the clock.

Across from him, Paddy fidgeted and asked, "Why aren't we moving? What's holding us up?"

"Us, for openers. Some other windows up and down the train no doubt got busted the same way."

Then the repair crew made a liar out of him and

got Paddy to fidget some more by dropping out of sight while the train still went on going no place. Paddy suddenly sat straighter with a gasp and said, "Oh, no! That man out there! He was one of the men who were tagging after me at El Paso!"

Longarm followed her gaze out the new glass to observe a foxy-faced individual, dressed cow, packing a low-slung six-gun and making his way across the tracks of the Monterrey yards in a sort of sidewinding slouch. Longarm said, "If he means to board this train he doesn't want too many folk to notice on the platform side. Are you sure he's one of your secret admirers and not just a vagabond gringo with a hankering to get to Mexico City?"

She shook her head and said, "I'd recognize that funny way he walks in the dark. They must have figured that since I wasn't on the one other railroad line I'd have to be on this one!"

As they lost sight of the sinister stranger Longarm rose, picked up their two bags, and said, "Let's go, then."

Paddy got to her feet, even as she asked him where they might be going. He said, "Out the other side, of course. This compartment's just off the front of this car. I'll go first and make sure the station platform is clear before we sort of hop off and let the rascal have the whole train to himself, see?"

She tagged along. She had little choice with him toting her bag, with that no doubt expensive forgery in it, but she protested, "I don't want to get off here in Monterrey, Custis. I don't *know* anyone in Monterrey!"

Longarm stuck his head out from between the cars to stare back the length of the platform. Except for some women and kids vending fruit and soda pop, the long platform seemed deserted and, even better, there was a doorway just a hop, skip, and jump away. So he told Paddy, "They just might know you have no sensible reason to visit Monterrey. So let's visit it and catch the next train south."

Then the one they were still on began to roll slowly forward and he added, "Let's *move* it, honey!"

So they did, and were inside, safe from view, as the other cars rolled on south, whether anyone was gazing out the windows or not.

Inside the musty smelling station, Paddy stared in dismay all about and protested, "This is dreadful! Why are all those ragged old men sprawled over all the benches?"

"This is a waiting room. Drunks who ain't going no place have to wait someplace. Follow me and I'll show you how to book a compartment right, for a change. You hired that last one under your true name, right?"

As she tagged after him she brightened and decided, "Oh, that must be how they knew I was on that train. The thought never crossed my mind, once I thought I'd eluded them at El Paso!"

Longarm didn't answer until he'd made it to the ticket window, put down their bags, and booked a compartment on the evening train for Señor y Señora Zubermacher. Then he picked up the bags to head for the baggage counter, saying, "There's heaps of German folk in Mexico right now and neither of us look all that Spanish."

She protested, "Don't check my bag, Custis.

We're deep in Old Mexico and I have a few valuables in there!"

But he went right on ahead, explaining, "There's much to be said for entrusting stuff to a railroad as executes engineers for running late. Them bags would be no safer if we try to carry 'em through the streets of Monterrey right now, and we'd attract more attention while we were at it."

He gave her claim check to her to stuff in her handbag and warned her to carry the same under her arm as if she was running for a football touchdown, or a rugby goal if she hadn't been keeping up to date on the sporting scene. But she was still fussing until they got outside and had to wade through raggedy-ass youths from six to sixty who seemed out to carry their bags if they had any or them if they hadn't. Longarm hung on to Paddy with one arm and bulled their way free of the mob around the railroad station to where they only passed a beggar every five or six paces. Downtown Monterrey was built up modern, which was to say cheap, and save the shabby peasant costumes of the more pestiferous Mex folk and "Viva La Revolución" chalked here and there, they could have been in any industrial slum from old Birmingham to, well, Monterrey. Paddy asked where all these noisy beggars could have come from. He explained they were country folk who should have never left the country, but added, "There ain't much of a future shucking another man's corn or chopping his cotton and they've heard of all the high-paying jobs in the steel mills, here. So here they are and here the jobs require at least a third- or fourth-grade education. El Presidente don't care. He'd *build* some school if he wanted him and his pals to pay servants more than room and leftovers."

He didn't think she wanted to hear how cheap a pretty teenaged virgin could be bought after her folk had gone hungry a spell in such a modernized country. He spied a hotel sign catty-corner across the street and got them both under cover before they got too far from the station. The fat lady behind the key counter was pleased to see Longarm had centavos to pay in advance, even if they had no baggage and la señorita was blushing more than she might have had they really been Señor y Señora Herrerro, as Smith was spelled in Spanish.

The room they wound up in on the third floor smelled of roach oil and jasmine-scented candles, but it had cross ventilation, and aside from the thin film of fly ash and soft-coal soot on the top quilt, the bedding seemed to be fresh. So Paddy proceeded to get undressed for bed.

Longarm said, "Hold the thought. I got to duck back out and buy us some disguises. But first we got some talking to do."

As she went right on stripping, sort of coyly, he lit a smoke and insisted, "Damn it, girl, I only came down here to pick up old T. J. Perkins, and now I seem to be enmeshed in all sorts of sneaky crap I don't have federal jurisdiction over even if I was all that interested. We've established that I like you downright scandalous, and I savvy that your pals in Mexico City might be able to put me back on T.J.'s trail. But every time I've asked for an infernal *name* so far, you've insisted on getting on top."

She sat almost nude on the bed to roll down her black lisle stockings as she asked him, with a lewd wink, if he'd rather get on top this time. He laughed despite himself and replied, "I said to hold the thought, you sweet little sass. All I know about you and your troubles so far is your name and the brand of your outfit up in San Miguel County, New Mexico Territory. I saw the fox-faced gent you seem to think the rascal out to take your land might have hired. Now tell me who in thunder the big land grubber is and just how big he might be."

She shrugged her naked shoulders to reply, "I have no secrets from you now, darling. The mean old brute who's out to diddle me out of my old homestead is Caleb Woodward of the W Bar W Land and Cattle Company. What difference might that make?"

Longarm whistled softly and said, "I've ridden through Santa Fe and you're right, he's big, and they say he's a hardnosed business cuss. If he was just another hard scrabble rancher we might be ducking friends and relations. A big shot like Woodward would hire the services of a professional outfit like the Pinks or the New Mexico Regulators. Henry McArthy, better known to innocent folk like you as Billy the Kid, used to ride for the Regulators before he went bad total. I hope we're dealing with the Pinks or the Burnes Agency. They got licenses to worry about. The Regulators are mean as well as professional. Not being bonded, they don't worry half as much about who they shoot it out with."

He took a thoughtful drag on his cheroot, then he asked, "What might the handle of your Mexico City law firm be, assuming I can get you there alive?"

She shot a string of Spanish names at him and added that their office was across from the municipal courthouse in downtown Mexico City. That figured and served to cheer him some. It was apt to take gents with such connections to root up old T.J. from amid the other lowlifes of a good-sized town where foreigners didn't stand out half as much as they might in a place like Nuevo Laredo.

He told Paddy to bar the door after him and not to let anyone but him back in. When she wailed about how helpless she'd be up there, all alone and unarmed, Longarm unclipped the derringer from the more sinister end of his watch chain and handed it to her as he snorted, "You'd think a lady traveling alone in Mexico or, hell, Kansas, would know enough to pack at least a .32 in her purse. Hang on to that *tight* if you have to shoot at anyone with it. It fires .44, twice, and kicks considerable for its size."

His words seemed to make her look more sick than assured. But he'd done all he could for her now. So he ducked out in the hall, waited until he heard her snick the big door bolt, and went back down to the street, knowing she was safe from anything short of a battering ram. Doors and door bolts were built solid down in Old Mexico. They had to be.

International Cable had offices all over and likely paid less taxes down this way. So, first things coming first, Longarm stopped by to fill in his home office on one of their blue blanks. He assured Billy Vail he was still searching for T. J. Perkins and didn't seem to be in any other trouble down this way. What Billy Vail didn't know wouldn't worry him, and the fat old cuss was sure a worrywart.

Finding a market square frequented by country folk was a mite tougher. All the new glass-fronted shops sold much the same duds as you'd see for sale in the same sort of shops in Denver. Once a Mex had a decent job he seemed to want to look like a gringo, even if he did say he just couldn't abide the breed. Longarm and Paddy were already dressed gringo. He was out to blur their outlines at a distance just a mite.

He headed upslope toward the older parts of town, figuring that was where things might still be sort of old-time traditional. The original Bishop's See and district capitol had been built in Spanish Imperial times atop a hill rising lonesome in the middle of a broad valley. Monterrey meant "King's Mountain." Since then the town had spread out from its original defensive position, without much city planning as far as Longarm could see. The infernal streets ran broad and narrow, straight and crooked, fairly flat and so steep the sidewalks were more like staircases. The railroad, wanting to run more level than a religious procession, had cut away the lower slopes between some newer and older parts of town to leave more Spanish-looking architecture perched atop a retaining wall so high that you had to scale a zigzag set of stone stairs to get up yonder. Longarm wanted to. So that was what he did, even though the sun was warming the whole place up now, wherever it might be above that sooty blanket of overcast. When he reached the top Longarm paused to get his breath as well as his bearings. Gazing down, he saw an ugly maze of tin-roofed factories in a cat's-cradle of connecting rail sidings. Tall chimneys in the middle to greater distance spewed yet more smoke. The other way, the street kept rising, cobblestoned, with walks to either side of those big blue bricks Spanish-speaking steel makers cast from spent iron-ore slag. The housing all about up here was built more traditional, with bitty barred windows and an occasional massive oak doorway facing the outside world. Hispanics lived inside-out from English-talking folk, with their gardens in the middle of their houses and nobody likely to invite themselves for lemonade on the front porch with the family unless they sent in a card and waited for an answer. It did make for privacy and no doubt avoided having to notice just how broke one's neighbors might be in a society where folk tended to live high on the hog or starve. There was just no way to tell if a Mex neighborhood was fancy or poor. So Longarm just kept going until, sure enough, he found awnings spread above stalls in the old cathedral plaza and tried not to notice the odd looks he got as the only gent dressed like him who seemed to be shopping that afternoon in this part of town. He bought a long black shawl for Paddy, made of machine-made lace for the campesino trade, and priced at what was small change for him and way too much for Mexican country folk. He rolled it up and stuffed it in a coat pocket. There was more air than mercerized cotton to the cheap lace.

He bought himself a dark straw sombrero and, not knowing what in thunder to do with his old Stetson, wadded the same up into the high crown of the Mex hat before he put it on. The old lady who'd sold it to him laughed at him, toothless, but didn't seem to care. Then he bought a serape that looked as if a drunken Navajo might have woven it from a machine-spun wool, dyed every color but sensible with German coal-tar dyes, and draped it over his left shoulder so it could hang down to cover the bulge his six-gun made under his frock coat. When he paused before a window just off the plaza to admire his outline, he saw he'd broken it pretty good. Up close he still looked like a gringo with mighty odd tastes in fashion. At any distance he might pass for a taller than average vaquero in town to get laid.

That reminded him of the great lay he had waiting for him down in the flatter parts of town and he just hated to run for trains without enjoying a smoke and a wash-up, after. So he spun on one heel to head back to that hotel a mite faster than he'd been poking about up to now.

He must have spun too suddenly for the sly-looking rascal gazing his way from the shady side of the plaza. It was that same fox-faced rascal Paddy had spotted out the train window. It seemed their ruse hadn't worked after all. They'd changed trains for no good reason. Longarm muttered, "All right, I've had just about enough of this sneaky shit!" and commenced to walk straight at the foxy sneak to see if he felt like fighting or talking. But the rascal didn't seem up to either, right now.

As he grasped Longarm's intent and went whipping around the nearest corner, he moved with that same odd walk. So Longarm called out, "You in the blue denims with the slithery stride! Hold still and stop slithering, damn it!"

But the mysterious cuss did no such thing and, by the time Longarm made it to the corner he'd ducked around, he was running like an apple thief down the steep and narrow street. So Longarm started running after him. Nobody in the blank-walled houses on either side seemed to give a damn.

It was easy to run fast, downhill. Staying on one's feet was trickier, slippery as those shiny blue slag bricks had been polished by many a bare foot since they'd been laid. But Longarm was gaining on his man as they both began to notice how the street came to a dead end at the cement railing of the retaining wall dividing this part of town from the rest, with a five- or six-story drop. Just in case anyone else might not have noticed, some thoughtful Mex had painted a sign warning, *"PELEGRO!"* and that reminded Longarm how dangerous a cornered rat could be as well. So he drew his .44-40 as he closed the distance between them, yelling, "Halt three times and I won't say four, you son of a bitch!"

The fugitive tried to stop and whirl with his own gun out as he got to the end of the dead-end street. Then his steel-tapped boot heel carried him like a spinning ice skater across the last blue bricks to crash his ass against the low guardrail. Then he wasn't there anymore, albeit he sure let out a yell on his way down.

Longarm slid to a safer stop, holstered his six-gun, and put both palms to the rough cement for a less noisy look-see over the edge. The cuss was sprawled on a railroad siding. Longarm could hardly ask him how he might feel from up here.

As he headed back up the slope an old lady popped open a door to throw a pail of slops on the already-slick-enough pavement. She caught Longarm's eye and asked, with a sad little shrug, what else she could do before they built that grand sewer they'd been talking about for years. He agreed housekeeping was mighty tedious and they parted friendly. It seemed obvious, now, that nobody had noticed what had just taken place out front. So Longarm knew he wasn't going to have to answer all sorts of tedious questions about a railroading accident. The only trouble was that he still had no idea who that other cuss had been, or why he'd been following Paddy's escort instead of Paddy, if that was the name of this fool game.

Chapter 3

Back at the hotel, Paddy was unable to shed further light on the subject, albeit the daylight coming through the slats of the window shutters sure shed interesting stripes of light across her bare behind as they conversed while going at it dog style. She kept saying he'd stop asking dumb questions and treat her right if he really liked what she was giving him. But he just pumped a mite faster as he replied, "I didn't know I was enjoying this all by myself, you sweet thing. I ain't trying to treat a lady rude, Paddy. It's just that there are times a man has worries on his mind no matter how grand he might be feeling. If that swan diver I just told you about was the only one who'd spotted us changing trains, we ought to be able to do this with more enthusiasm on the next train, after dark. The question is whether he was working alone and, if not, with how many and do they have the station staked out."

She chewed one corner of the pillow under her spread-out brown tresses as she sort of moaned, "Listen to him, Mother Venus, he's got me right on the edge with his yardstick measuring my deepest secrets and he wants to talk about choo-choo trains and, oh, Jeeezuss, *faster*, Custis, faster!"

That made two of them. But once they'd come and were able to converse more sensibly, cuddled atop the bedding to share an al fresco smoke, even if they were indoors, Longarm said, "I want you to think back. You said you'd spotted that gimp-walking gent tailing you in and about El Paso. What might anyone with him have looked like, and how big a gang are we talking?"

She snuggled closer and began to toy with the hair on his bare chest as she replied thoughtfully, "More than three but fewer than, say, half a dozen. You know how it is when you try to tally stock without having time to count."

He nodded and said, "Right. Crows and human beings can count to three without moving their lips. After that you just have to count on purpose. Back home we used to fool crows like that. If three of us kids moved in near a crows' roost, the old crows could tell if two of us came out, leaving one behind with a ten gauge. But we found they couldn't tell if five of us went in and only four came out. You did single out that foxy face and funny walk as went with one of 'em. What can you recall about one or more of the others?"

She began to twist hairs thoughtfully as well as lower down as she decided, "Well, all of them looked big and rough to me. But I suppose a big tough man like you might not have been as impressed. Let's agree they were all dressed cow and average-sized or bigger. Does that help, darling?"

He placed the tip of the cheroot between her lips as he said, "Not as much as it might if you remembered something more distinct, and leave my poor thing alone right now. This other trouble you got me mixed up in sounds more serious. Less fun, at any rate. A crew of gents dressed Americano might be

40

easier to spot at some distance, which is why I brung home that serape and sombrero for me and enough lace to hide your light brown hair for you. But I can't just throw down on any bunch of gringo cow hands I bump noses with, lest they turn out to be a musical quartet."

He took the cheroot back for a thoughtful drag before he went on, "What puzzles me most is what *point* any number of hired guns might have in following you about so mysterious."

She tried, "Maybe they're afraid I'll do something about that fake land grant Caleb Woodward claims he has on file in Ciudad Mejico, dear."

"I just said that. If your land-hungry neighbor wanted you dead he'd have had you bushwhacked on your own range to begin with. So that can't be it, and old fox-faced was tailing me, not you, this afternoon."

She snuggled even closer to say, "I have lots of friends up in San Miguel County, you know."

He cuddled her back to say dryly, "I figured you must have lots of friends back home, you friendly little thing. But even saying a less popular cattle baron might not want to risk calming you down on your own sweet stomping ground, they had the chance to do you dirt in El Paso and just settled for scaring you. I'd say they're waiting for you to make some move of your own before they move in on you. I doubt old Caleb Woodward cares how popular you make yourself in Mexico City, as long as you don't get too near the hall of records there. But, damn it, that don't work so hot either."

She asked why and he explained, "By the time Woodward ever saw fit to challenge your old Spanish

41

land grant with another, he must have known exactly what was on file in Mexico City. He has to have lawyers as well as gunslicks on his payroll. It would only take any lawyer worth his salt one afternoon at the most to paw through the files and see whether his claim is the real one or not. If I had old family records filed with the Mex government, I'd have long since had 'em verified by a paid-up Mexico City Notary Public. So why hasn't Woodward?"

She began to twist body hairs indeed as she replied wistfully, "He has. The papers he presented against me at the Santa Fe courthouse were from a Mexican law firm working for him. They were a modern copy of the original grant, certified as such by a Mexican notary who claims above his seal to have read them in or about the old hall of records."

Then she started kissing her way down his belly, trailing her questing fingernails with her lush lips, as he groaned, "Oh, hell, nothing makes a lick of sense. Whether his claim is fake or your claim is fake, he has to know it and—Hold on, maybe that's it. Lawyers have been known to lie and have it notarized. If it's all a bluff on his part he wouldn't want you poking through that hall of records with or without lawyers paid to lie for you."

She didn't answer. She must have considered it impolite to try and talk with her mouth full. He laughed, growled, "Waste not, want not," and rolled her on her back to finish right.

That sure served to kill some more of the afternoon. But later he felt obliged to tell her, "As I was saying before I was so rudely interrupted, I just can't let you go anywhere near that hall of records, honey."

That got her attention, even if she did have her bare heels hooked over his naked shoulders. She protested, "But I *have* to! That's the whole point of this long business trip, dear!"

He moved in her teasingly, not wanting to argue with a lady, as he insisted, "That's just what they don't want you doing and they're sure to have the hall of records staked out. But they might not know me on sight and can't have any orders about me. A federal lawman could have all sorts of good reasons to visit the hall of records at the capitol. I'm tougher than you if they don't see it that way, and my badge can get me in at times they'd feel no call to be watching for anybody to try. They'll only want to stake the place out during hours it's open to the general public, so, right, I'll be proud to just slip in and, ah, what am I supposed to do then, Paddy?"

She seemed unaware how she was moving in time with his thrusts as she answered, "Nothing. There's nothing I could ask a lawman of your rep to do back among those old record books and— Oh, good heavens, now you have me doing it, too! Are we supposed to be fornicating or conversing, you idiot?"

He laughed and moved faster in her, but kept his voice conversational as he said, "Old pals can do both. That's why it's so nice to be in bed with old pals. There's this one gal in Denver I've been seeing some time and she thinks it's sort of fun to ask me what I'd like for dinner when we wake up sort of pals in the morning."

She closed her eyes to tell him, through clenched teeth, not to be so beastly. Then she popped them open to stare up at him, demanding, "You don't ever intend to tell anyone about *us*, do you?"

He chuckled fondly and assured her as he humped her, "I failed to mention that other lady's name, just now, didn't I? Far be it from me to cast one shadow on the reputation I feel sure you must enjoy in San Miguel County. About me sneaking into that hall of records in your place—"

"It's not *true!*" she cut in, really starting to bounce under him as she sobbed, "I don't screw every man I meet and I make my hired hands call me ma'am at all times. You can't go to the hall of records for me. I have to go myself."

He said, "I was wondering how come you didn't have anyone with pants and a gun backing your play until you ran across me. I'd hate to ride for a female boss who treated me different than the other ranchers, too, come to study on it. Maybe we ought to study on that. Are you certain any and all your family retainers back home are on your payroll and no other payroll worth mention?"

She sort of groaned, "Getting to my hired help wouldn't do Caleb Woodward any good. My God, I just *came*, while I was in the middle of a sentence!"

He kissed her and said, "Me too, ain't it fun? I hope you see, now, that grabbing at me every time I try to ask sensible questions just don't work, Paddy. I'm paid to be a questioning pest. I just like to come because it feels so much better than smoking. If you want me to come in you some more you're going to have to start talking pard-to-pard with me. For fibbing is the one sin I won't go along with, and I'd as soon track T. J. Perkins down all by myself as wander about Old Mexico with a moving target who can't seem to trust me and vice versa."

"Don't take it out yet. If you must know, I've

been planning to replace just one little page in an old musty record book with a page of my own. The lawyer who managed to get it for me says half the old bindings are loose and that nobody pays any attention as long as you spend plenty of time back among the old stacks and don't seem to be carrying anything *out* with you."

So, having confirmed what he'd already figured out, and seeing he seemed to have her leveling with him at last, Longarm did his level best to make her come some more and she acted grateful as hell about that.

Later, she confessed she had the fake land grant in her bag at the station. He acted surprised and said, "You know I can't be party to criminal fraud, even in a country run by criminals. But, as I keep telling wayward youths I get to arrest a lot, you'd be surprised how often honesty can be the best policy. So here's what we're going to do. Once we get to the capitol, Lord willing and we don't get shot, I mean to scout the hall of records ahead of you. If I see it's easy to get in and out, and that nobody wants to gun me or read over my shoulder as I go through them old Spanish ledgers, we'll just take her from there."

She protested, "What good will that do me if you're too honest to fiddle the records for me, dear?"

He rolled one of her nipples between thumb and forefinger to show he was still on her side as he said, "For openers, we won't know any records need to be fiddled until I take a look at 'em. Wouldn't you feel silly paying for a forgery if all the time it was someone other than your great grandfather that was lying to begin with?"

• • •

The rest of their journey to Ciudad Mejico was un-eventful, unless one felt like calling that experiment Paddy wanted to try with that mailing tube an event. Longarm found it just sort of silly.

It was still dark when their night train rolled in. He still led her from the yards by way of a fence he had to boost her over, in case anyone was watching the regular ways out to the street at such an ungodly hour. Longarm had been there before. So she only got to walk far enough to bitch a mite before he had her bedded down again in a small, clean, and hope-fully discreet posada that usually catered only to Mexicans just in from the country. One such gent who stayed there when he was in town was a rebel leader called El Gato. Having quietly evoked the pro-fessional name of his somewhat boisterous but faith-ful old friend, Longarm figured they'd be discreet as hell. There were times when having friends in *low* places could serve a gringo better than having them in high places, down this way.

Paddy seemed to be feeling the effects of all the beds she'd been in since they'd met. She flopped wearily down but asked him, shyly, if he'd really mind if she just went to sleep. She said she knew men never bought that story about a lady having a headache, but that though her head just felt dopey, there were parts of her that were really starting to feel bruised.

He chuckled fondly and moved over to the win-dow seat with even his hat still on, saying, "I told you that trick with the mailing tube would hurt. You just go on and catch some well-deserved rest, pard. I'd be lying if I said I had better places to go right now, but I still have to go, as soon as the streets get more crowded. Strangers creeping through the dawn's early light attract attention, even when they ain't creeping."

She didn't answer. She was already fast asleep. She sure did lack endurance for such a horny little gal. He didn't feel like talking to anybody right now in any case. He'd just about talked himself dry without getting enough sensible answers to matter.

He lit a cheroot as he sat there gazing out the window from the unlit room they'd holed up in. The sky was commencing to lighten and the top-story digs afforded him a view of the distant looming mass to the southwest. It was the only hill rising above a dead-flat city built mostly on the bottom of a now-dry lake bed. The Aztec had named it Chapultepec, meaning grasshopper hill, and none of the many folk who'd used it since had seen fit to give it another name. Chapultepec had been many things to many Mexicans, starting with the Halls of Montezuma, or Aztec palace, up yonder. Cortez had torn most of those walls down, of course. At the time of the Mexican War there'd been a military academy atop the rise, Mexico's answer to West Point. Longarm raised his free right hand in a stiff cavalry salute to the dark brooding mass as he thought about that. For a heap of good men, on both sides, had died fighting for their two countries on the rocky heights of Chapultepec.

When old Winfield Scott marched into Mexico City, the young military cadets up yonder had run up the eagle and tricolor of Mexico and dared el yanqui to do his damndest. So the U.S. Marines had gotten a fine battle hymn and a heap of casualties out of the scrap they'd had over the Halls of Montezuma. The teenaged boys holding the heights had made liars out of anyone who said greasers couldn't fight, as well. For they'd fought to the last man, then *he'd* died like a man whether he was old enough to shave regular or not. The marines had been pinned down good amid the rocks and never would have made it to the top if the army artillery hadn't pitched in to help a heap more than that tribute to the marines allowed.

Longarm's introspective mood was broken by a donkey car wailing its wheels down below. He saw shadowy figures on their way to work as well. He nodded, stood up, and went downstairs looking Mexican as he could manage in his serape and sombrero. He circled some to make sure he wasn't being followed before he headed for the center of town.

A sign out front of the hall of records said the place just didn't open until nine. Longarm cast a look around, didn't see anyone else close enough to matter, and proceeded to pound the door with enthusiasm. After he'd about worn himself out at that the caretaker he knew they had to have inside cracked the door open far enough to tell Longarm he couldn't dammit come in this early. But he seemed impressed by Longarm's badge and credentials, whether he could read them or not. So he sighed, let the infernal gringo in, but said, "I fear I can be of no service to you. I know little or nothing about the records stored here. Perhaps if you would like to wait until one of the officials arrives, let us say around nine?"

Longarm shook his head and replied, "This matter is of vital importance to both your government and mine. I know what I'm here to verify. Just show me where old Spanish land grants might be kept and I can do the rest, viejo."

The old man shrugged, told Longarm to follow him, and led the way up some stairs and way the hell back through the building of considerable size. He unlocked a door to let out some cobwebs and mummy-dust scented air, saying, "Excuse the dust, por favor. We dare not open the windows, and open flames are forbidden in this part of the building as well. Some of the books date back to the times of Cortez and go poof if one holds a candle anywhere near them."

Longarm said the light through the grimy windows would do him fine. The old man shrugged and went back down to do whatever old men did alone in buildings full of dust. It took Longarm some time to figure how the old Spanish record books were stacked. Once he had, it took less time to find a binding allowing its contents might have dealings with land titles way up north in Nuevo Mejico. New Mexico Territory hadn't been named as such by Americans after they'd taken it away from Old Mexico. Mexico had simply taken it away from Indians after they already had a regular old Mexico, which was close enough to what the Indians down this way had called at least some of it.

The volume was big as well as heavy. Once Longarm had it on a handy windowsill, having opened it gingerly to keep it from crumbling to dust in his hands, he saw they'd been smart enough to bind the separate sheets of what looked and felt like charred pasteboard in alphabetical order. When he turned to where great grandfather O'Boyne's land grant should have been, it just wasn't there. There wasn't any *W* in the Spanish alphabet and Caleb Woodward wouldn't have any land grant he'd bought off a poor

Mex family filed under his own name in any case. Longarm swore and started to close the book. He'd naturally asked Paddy the name that might appear on any rival grant. But she hadn't known it, cuss her sweet hide. Then Longarm had a better idea. He just started gingerly turning pages and damned if they didn't have O'Boyne listed under the *B*'s instead of the *O*'s. He chuckled and muttered, "Sure, to an old Spanish scribe, the *O* would seem just a title, like La or De, whether he knew what an Irish *O*' meant or not. It's *us* as consider an *O*' or a Mac the start of a name."

He gently tugged at the binding. The O'Boyne grant was stuck in the book good. That meant it had been there some time or that some forger was just so slick it was sickening. Longarm scanned the spidery script through its film of age and neglect. The Spanish was too fancy, likely antique, for him to follow with any ease. But it sure seemed to say that one Tomas O'Boyne, as they spelled Thomas, had done wonders and ate cucumbers for the king of Spain in a fuss he'd had with the English one time. That made sense, for a wild goose named O'Boyne. So Paddy's land grant was the real thing. Someone had been out to flimflam her just as bold as brass. But how could they have hoped to get away with anything as brass-balled as this?

He closed the old volume and gently put it back where he'd found it, muttering, "All right. Say a greedy cattle baron took a notion to check out the grant of a neighbor, having heard she held her land more by tradition than a proper U.S. deed. Say a sloppy lawyer made the mistake I almost managed and so he wired Woodward the O'Boynes never got

50

acre-one from any king of Spain? He'd have known she had a copy on file up New Mexico way, but since he thought it a fake, he found it just as fair to fake one of his own, and where does that leave us?"

He couldn't answer that. He went out to the hall and started searching for a way out. Before he found one, the same old-timer found him. The custodian was not alone, now. He had a fussy gent in a linen suit and two Mex lawmen in uniform with him. It was the dude in the suit who insisted they search Longarm.

Longarm let them. He had nothing to hide, and when one asked him for why he kept a yanqui hat in the crown of his straw sobrero, Longarm just asked the Mex lawmen where *else* they wanted him to keep it. So they just laughed, sort of amused by the strange ways of el gringo, and the curator calmed down some when they told him Longarm didn't seem to be trying to sneak anything out of the place. The fussy Mex read Longarm's credentials more carefully the second time, and asked grudgingly, "Very well, if you are a lawman and not a ladrone, after all, just what have you been up to here?"

Longarm told him truthfully, "I wanted to verify a land grant." Then, since truth didn't have to cause needless trouble, he said, "The Irvine Grant near San Diego, California, is being disputed by some gent as wants to build a railroad across it."

He'd no sooner said that than he saw he'd put his foot in it. But the dapper Mex didn't ask what the original Spanish name on that famous grant might have been. He just looked pained and said, "Nobody, pero *nobody*, can dispute one of those old royal grants. Is a matter of international treaty as well as

51

tradition! You should have come to me, first. I could have saved you and our precious records the wear and tear!"

Longarm agreed he'd been hasty and asked, "Just what do you do when somebody comes to you with such a dispute? Surely they must do that often, land being so valuable today, and the old Spanish kings being so generous in doling out the same."

The curator shrugged and said, "It does not happen often. As you should have known, visitors are supposed to consult with me before they come up here. In all modesty, I happen to be an expert on old documents. I can tell at a glance, or prove it with laboratory tests if I must, whether any document we have stored with us is genuine or not. They do not, for example, make ink or sealing wax to the same formula used a mere hundred years ago by the Spanish court."

Longarm didn't care to know what the Spanish court was using recently. So he nodded soberly and said, "I'll tell my government how expert you are," which inspired the curator to even smile as he whipped out his card for Longarm to carry back to the states with him. Longarm gravely put it away. The cuss might still come in handy if he was missing something here. On the face of it, Woodward still had to be cursed, or blessed, with balls of brass.

Later, back at the posadal, Longarm told Paddy what he'd found out at the hall of records and added, "I told you honesty could be the best policy, if you don't overdo it. Had you tried to get away with that dumb forgery, you'd have been caught by that dumb *O*' being where a Spanish scribe would say the name began with a *B*."

She gulped, sitting bare in bed, and said, "Never mind all that. Thanks to you we can just tear up the fake I paid good money for and streak back home to ask Caleb Woodward just what on earth he was trying to pull on us!"

Longarm took off his hat and coat, sat on that same window seat and mildly observed, "*We* ain't mutual victims of your land-hungry neighbor. I'm down here to pick up T. J. Perkins and transport him back to one of the many courts as want to try him for crimes too numerous to mention. But *you* better do some streaking for home, Paddy. I've done some thoughtful walking just now. The hall of records is a fair walk from here. Ponder as I might, I can't come up with any way anyone could have really planned to steal your land. You got your own grant filed in Santa Fe, it matches the one Mexico's been holding for you all this time, and since they make *me* sign everything in triplicate, I wouldn't bet on there not being a copy in the Royal Archives over in Madrid, if I was out to flimflam anyone with my own sneaky penmanship. I doubt old Woodward even tried to fiddle the records here in Old Mexico. He might have hoped you'd get caught fiddling them so he could take you to court in New Mexico Territory with both of you standing on legs too shaky for a gringo judge and jury to fathom."

He reached in his shirt pocket for a smoke as he added, "On the other hand, he could have set you up to play chess when the name of the game was checkers. He might not be the least bit interested in stealing your *land*."

She stared up at him like a naked owl to demand, "Then why on earth have I been put to all this time and expensive trouble if nobody can get at my land after all?"

Longarm lit his cheroot, shook out the match, and asked her mildly, "What do you raise on all that New Mexico range, horny toads?"

She gasped, "Ohmygod! Fall roundup starts next month, too! Are you saying it's my *herd* he's really after?"

Longarm shrugged and said, "You said Woodward's new in the territory, and beef stock's selling two dollars higher this summer, if I read the financial pages of the *Denver Post* at all correct. You've told me you make your hired hands call you ma'am and I'll take your word you don't kiss 'em all that often. With you wandering mysterious, clean out of the country, how hard would you reckon anyone might be guarding your cows, without even being ordered to by anyone in total charge?"

She said that had to be it and patted the sheets beside her as she added he was smart as hell. He just blew smoke out his nostrils like an old bull studying on which way to charge and answered, "Hell, I could be dumb, for all we really know. I told you I just took a long walk with my fool head all abuzz. The notion someone's as likely after your stock as your land is only one of the better notions I buzzed up. It works, for you, at least, and I might feel less confounded if I only had one crook at a time to ponder. So we'd best put you on a northbound train and I'll wire the U.S. marshal in Santa Fe to meet you at the station and hear your tale of woe. Stealing stock and herding the same through a federal territory is a federal offense and I know the Santa Fe bunch personal, so—"

"I can't go back all that way without an armed escort!" she cut in with a wail. "You said yourself they might still be watching me! What good will it do my poor cows if I never make it even as far as the border alive?"

He grimaced and growled, "When you're right you're right. Sort of. But if murder was on old Woodward's mind, they had plenty of chances to do you before now, and they didn't. I sure wish I was a mind reader. Just trying has me mighty confused."

He flicked ashes out the window and went on, "Did you ever hear the joke about the new parson in town who meets up with this sweet little gal setting on the steps out front with a big old redbone hound? No? Well, the parson asks the kid if her dog bites and she allows with a smile of pure innocence that her dog's never bit nobody yet. So the parson goes to pet the ugly mutt and it damn near tears his arm off. Next time he comes across the little sass, with his arm in a sling, he demands to know how come she assured him so sweet that her dog never bit, to which she demurely replies that the one as bit him wasn't her dog."

Paddy didn't laugh. She asked him what on earth jokes about little girls and big dogs had to do with the fix they seemed to be in. He took another drag and explained, "We could be jumping to conclusions like that parson. Meeting up with sinister plotters goes with my job. Nobody likes to go to jail, and while I don't like to brag, I enjoy a rep for putting folk in jail. At the moment I'm on the trail of a murderous international jewel thief and if he doesn't know that, or that I know him on sight, now, he's got no business leading such an uncertain life. Thanks to you and that slippery Mex lawyer, Gomez, he got out of the jail they were supposed to be holding him in for me. But he must have more friends than that in Mexico. His yellow sheets describe him as operating mostly south of the border, and he only got into that shoot-out in New Orleans trying to smuggle stolen goods where such plunder can be sold for more. You could have been mistaken about that gent pestering us in Monterrey. He could have been after *me* all the time. He wasn't nowheres near you when he fell off that retaining wall, you know."

She seemed to be thinking sincerely before she shook her head firmly and insisted, "I'm sure I saw him earlier in El Paso. How could he and those others have expected to meet *you* there if that was who they were after?"

Longarm sighed and decided, "I can't say for sure he was after anybody. He commenced to run from me the moment I went after him."

He got out a notepad and a stub pencil as he told her, "I want to write down the name and address of that law firm your own lawyer back home put you on to. I don't want to forget it, and you did say Gomez said they'd be able to root out T. J. Perkins for me, right?"

She rolled off the bed and padded bare-assed to get at her handbag. The view was inspiring, going and coming. She likely knew it. As she handed Longarm a business card she told him coyly, "You don't have to write it down, darling. Just stick this in your pocket and then stick something nicer in me in the time I just saved you."

He laughed, hugged her against his bulging pants with one arm as he used the other to put the business card away, and told her, "You didn't save us nearly the time to do that right and you know it. I'll be back as soon as I can manage to take you up on such a kind offer. But if you really want me to carry you back to New Mexico you're going to have to let me catch old T.J. first."

She grimaced and asked, "Does that disgusting little man have to travel all the way with us, dear?"

"Depends on him. If he won't come quiet he may get to make the journey in the baggage car, in a box."

Chapter 4

Americano law firms labeled their doors confusing compared to those south of the border. They didn't throw in their mothers' as well as their fathers' names, connected by *y*. The offices that went with the card cluttered with Mexican names that Paddy had given Longarm were imposing, and faced the old baroque cathedral across a big barren plaza. Longarm had to wait a spell in the reception room before he found this out, of course. The snippy receptionist acted as if she thought she was at least the queen of Spain, and insisted on showing off her piss-poor English by refusing to understand Longarm's fair-to-middling Spanish. After she'd made him listen to her typewriter playing for a million years she decided one of her bosses would see him. So he followed her along a mile of crimson corridor carpet to a massive oaken door carved for the grating of massive cheese, and showed him into a sort of plush torture chamber.

Two suits of armor, hopefully hollow, stared at him from the same number of corners. Maces, battle-axes, and swords, lots of swords, were hung all over the ivory-plaster walls. The ominously heavy-looking oak ceiling was a much bigger version of the cheese-grater door, only the massive crossbeams were pinned together with spikes bigger than the Union Pacific held its tracks down with, and Longarm suddenly recalled that this was earthquake country.

But the old gent seated behind an acre or so of desk with a coat of arms above his head and a swell view of the cathedral to his right didn't look as if he ever worried about anything. His handshake was friendly as his gilt-edged smile. He sat his American visitor down on a big oak chair between desk and window, slid a cigar humidor Longarm's way, and asked what else he could do for him.

Longarm reached for one of those dollar cigars—he was no fool—as he said, "Well, Señor, ah, Lopez—?"

"Lopez y Morales, por favor. I am directly descended from Marin Lopez, who rode with Cortez, and Fidel Morales, who was of course the then-humble crossbowman who founded the ranchero dynasty I'm sure you must have heard so much about."

Longarm said dryly, "Oh, *those* Morales folk. You surely have a swell family tree. If we could get back to the here and now, I hope your associate, Gomez, wired you that I was on my way here with La Señorita Patricia O'Boyne of Nuevo Mejico."

The older man nodded soberly and said, "He did. I must say I found his message disturbing. But by the time we could wire back the two of you had already left. There was no good reason for la señorita to journey so far, with or without an escort. We were able to determine at once that the O'Boyne land grant was authentic and, say what you will of my ancestors, iron-clad and idle to dispute."

Longarm finished lighting his cigar. It had taken some doing. He knew better than to keep his own tobacco in a damned old jar with a wet sponge. It sure tasted good, once you got it going, though. He said as much and added, "She tells me her business rival waved a notarized deposition from another Mexican law firm at her, just before she lit out for Mexico. That was why she felt she ought to."

The dignified old coot looked disgusted and replied, "We know all about that. The petty crook who got a tobacco-shop notary for to put his X on such worthless paper is, alas, well known to us. I knew at once they were trying to pull, how you say, blankets, over the poor child's eyes. The attorney retained here by that Woodward person would blanket his own father's eyes for money, if he knew who his father might be. He should have been disbarred long ago. Alas, the political situation down here does not provide for disbarring lawyers just for being unethical. My country needs outside investors and they in turn seem to find it easier to set up here with crooked lawyers."

Longarm decided the old gent could be forgiven some of his snooty ways if they made him look down on the less than pure Spanish Diaz and his courthouse gang. He nodded and said, "I told la señorita I thought it looked as if she'd been sent on a snipe hunt. I doubt her cows will miss her, or vice versa, this side of roundup time, when lots of cows turn up missing if nobody's there to ask questions as strange riders push strange cows all over the place. So tell me something else, as long as we got her old Spanish grant out of the way. What might have happened to, ah, anyone who got caught pussyfooting about the hall of records with fake documents, as if they might be out to fiddle with recorded history just a mite?"

The old Mex lawyer looked shocked and answered flatly, "They would most definitely spend a very long time in court, if not even longer in prison. I know what they say about our current form of government, in your country, Señor Long. One learns to be patient by the time one has seen as many Mexican governments come and go as I have. Things may be a bit, ah, unsettled here at the moment, but there are limits. Forgery is a most serious offense in La Republica, unless you get approval in advance, at any rate."

Longarm nodded and said, "That's what I figured. The ruse was meant to keep folk's mind off beef on the hoof for quite a spell. So I'd best get la señorita safely home and turn her case over to the Santa Fe marshal while she still *has* said beef on the hoof."

He took another luxurious drag on the fancy cigar and added, "I can't go anywhere until I pick up the crook they sent me south to pick up in the first place. Gomez told la Señorita that you and your pals could help me with that, knowing the underbelly of such a big town so much better than me."

The older man looked as if he'd just caught his only daughter fooling around with the butler as he protested, "Gomez had no right to tell anyone that! I'll have you know we are an old and most respectable firm and I don't think Gomez will ever work with us again!"

Longarm said soothingly, "It's my understanding La Señorita O'Boyne's Santa Fe lawyer put her on to Gomez as a border-town fixer who knew everybody worth knowing. I can see why you might have found him useful in the past. Are you saying he just plain lied when he said you boys could put me on to that slippery T. J. Perkins' trail?"

The older man shrugged and said, "He must have. He sent us no word concerning anyone named Perkins. He told us he was trying to help la señorita prove her just claims to her family land grant and asked if we could help. It was no problem at all. I simply sent one of my law clerks to the hall of records and we got off a verification to Nuevo Laredo that very day. It should be there by now."

Longarm grimaced and said, "Well, you know how impatient some women get. Can we stick to how in thunder I'm supposed to catch up with old T.J. on my very own?"

The honest lawyer, if such existed, sighed and said, "Gomez might have assumed we stooped to the level of that other firm the young woman's rival contacted. When one is not skilled enough at statute law to win fairly, in court, one may be just a bit inclined to stoop to false witnesses, arresting officers whose memory can change for money, unethical bail-bondsmen and so forth, eh?"

Longarm smiled thinly and said, "Now *that* sounds like the sort of lawyer I'm looking for. Might you know the name and address of those crooks Woodward's crooked lawyer contacted here in your otherwise fair city?"

The older man grimaced and said, "They are called Robles, Robles y Robles. Only our one true God knows if they dare to do business under their true names. They are in the city directory. We have no occasion to deal with such vile people. I think I heard their office is near the *cárcel municipal*."

Longarm nodded and said, "The neighborhood of the city jail is where you find such lawyers in my country, too. It's been nice talking to you, Señor. But now I have to go talk to the sort of outfit Gomez must have had in mind."

The older man nodded soberly and said, "I wish you wouldn't call such people *lawyers*. Has it occurred to you that since they have been retained by that Woodward scoundrel, they might not want to work for you?"

Longarm nodded back, grimmer, to say, "It ain't as if I mean to give 'em much choice in the matter."

Like any big city, the one called Mexico City was a patchwork of decent, halfway decent, and downright god-awful parts. City jails were seldom built in fancy residential neighborhoods, so Longarm was expecting to find Robles, Robles y Robles set up in a slum. But when he got there he decided they'd overdone it a mite. The narrow street reeked of horseshit, human piss, beans, pepper, tobacco, as well as marijuana and cheap perfume. He had to ask directions. In the end a shitty little kid wearing nothing but a shitty shirt led Longarm to a sort of hole-in-the-wall staircase, didn't thank him for the centavos, and left him on his own. Longarm studied the signs running up the steep stairs, and they finally informed him that if he didn't need a love potion, a palm reading, or a swell massage from a certified virgin, there was a law firm on the top floor—and the infernal building was six stories tall. He hoped it was built of baked brick instead of adobe as he climbed the rickety stairs.

Robles, Robles y Robles had the whole top floor to themselves, and it wasn't as bad as it could have been once he ducked inside, out of the bean and piss fumes. A downright pretty señorita, if you liked 'em plump and busty with roses in their hair, greeted him sweet enough, but said there were only two gents called Robles working there and that they were both in court right now. He asked what they'd been accused of. She didn't smile. She'd no doubt heard that before. It seemed pretty obvious when one gazed about. The front office was dinky and dingy, and the framed diplomas on the rough stucco walls could have been fishing licenses for all Longarm could tell. The gal had been seated at a dinky blue table when he'd entered, but she'd sprung up in surprise, or terror, when he'd flashed his badge at her. She moved sort of graceful for a gal who obviously enjoyed eating so much. At the rate she was going she'd be downright fat by the time she was thirty. At the moment she seemed about twenty-odd and sort of cream-puff yummy. But he reminded himself that wasn't what he'd come all this way for, as he'd assured those other gals down in the street. So he said, "I really need your services bad. Maybe if I was to just drift over to the court—"

But she cut in, firmly, "Pero no. Is a most important case. The defendant really *did* it. Might el señor be too proud for to accept legal advice from a mere woman?"

It wouldn't have been polite to tell her she didn't look all that mere to him. So he said, "I sure need advice from somebody. Are you saying you're a sort of lady lawyer, Señorita, ah . . .?"

"Robles," she replied. "I do not appear in court. I do not enjoy being laughed at by illiterates. Pero I do hold a degree in Mexican law. Ambitious as well as kind parents sent me as well as my two brothers to the university, just before the government closed it.

Before we go on, I must tell you our fee for consultation is fifty pesos."

Longarm said that sounded fair and didn't add how cheap it might be by American standards. He paid her in real money with lower numbers printed in the corners and she said, "Bueno. Let us go back to the terrace where it may not be so stuffy, eh?"

He followed her. Most men would have, given any reason at all to do so. She swung her well-upholstered seat like a saloon door on payday. He was surprised when they got there to see they'd set out tin tables and chairs atop the flat roof of the next building over, shaded by an awning and planted with greenery in big clay pots. She sat him right down and poured him some passion-flower juice before taking her own seat across from him and breaking out a legal pad and pencil. By this time they'd established she was a Rosalinda as well as a Robles. He told her she could call him Custis. But she called him Deputy Long as she wrote that down and asked him what in thunder he wanted.

He said, "Since honesty has been doing right by me, up to now, I'd best fill you in from the beginning."

So he did. He noticed she wasn't writing anything down, and by the time he'd gotten to his visit at the other law firm, she looked as if she wanted her drink back.

There was no wholesome way he could offer to return the passion-flower juice he'd drunk so far, so he swallowed the last of it and said, "There you have it. I have to carry that other pretty gal back to the U.S. of A., and I can't do that until I catch up with the crook Tio Sam wants me to bring back as well. Your turn."

Rosalinda Robles shook her head and said, "Pero no, it would be most unethical for to take your case. If would be a, how you say, conflict of interests? One of my brothers has been dealing with Señor Caleb Woodward's Americano firm. But as I do most of the typing I am familiar with the situation. For how could we help you and that Americana when Señor Woodward has retained us to dispute her claim to his land in Nuevo Mejico?"

"Easy," Longarm said. "To begin with, assuming you and your brothers are stupid instead of unethical, Woodward has no claim on said land. It's been in another family for centuries and I don't want to argue about that. If you'd really done more than take his money and send him worthless paper you figured he'd like to read to a gringo judge who can't get at you, you'd know that. So ethic me no ethics and let's get down to how many other usefully shady characters you might know."

She told him, tight-lipped, to take his money back and go somewhere else, anywhere else, before her big brother Ramon got back. Apparently Ramon had a temper and didn't like to be made out a crook. Longarm asked, "What's wrong with him if he ain't a crook, then? Might he just be a lazy cuss with a drinking problem?"

She didn't answer. But he could see by the way she was blushing that he'd sent that one into the black if not the bulls-eye.

He nodded to say more gently, "Lots of gents who just can't concentrate on paperwork when they're dry take the easy way for a modest fee, Rosalinda. I'm sure that mean gringo lawyer had your brother convinced they had the goods on La Señorita O'Boyne and just needed verification. The hall of records is a long walk from here and I noticed, just now, that you can have anything you want notorized just down the street while you're waiting for a haircut."

She looked away, off across the rooftop of the big low-slung city, murmuring, "Please go. We do not wish for any trouble."

He took one of her plump hands gently in his, but left an edge to his voice as he replied, "You're already in trouble. Ramon got stinko and fiddled with official records, assuming I take your word on that. It gets worse if he did so sober. But I ain't out to put an already hardscrabble outfit out of business, Rosalinda. I don't think much of the law down here when they're trying to do things legal. I'm only pointing out that your law firm is crooked because I need a crooked lawyer, see?"

She must not have. She snatched her hand back and insisted, "There is nothing we can do for you. I swear I never heard the name of this Perkins person before you mentioned it just now!"

"I'll take your word on that, with a pinch of salt at any rate. But you and your brothers deal all the time with the underworld of this big town. You have to know lots of shady folk to stay in business. The fugitive I'm tracking just hit town with a modest bankroll and me right on his tail. Men in that fix don't check into the Grand Hotel, or even a posada that asks its guest to register. Mex law requires any licensed posada to keep a record of folk that check in and out. We both know one can get around that, for a price. T.J. had been locked up a spell when that Gomez gent bailed him out ahead of me, so he'd likely want strong drink and weak women to catch up with as well. I just got here and I know eight out of ten streetwalkers in this town have to be police informers. Nobody's allowed to do that much business free of any government supervision. So you know what I'm getting at, Rosalinda. I need to be put in touch with the same sort of folk I'd want to know if I was an Americano stranger on the run and didn't want to get picked up sleeping in one of your parks or railroad stations, right?"

She said softly, "I know the sort of people you mean. We do defend some receivers of stolen property or vendors of a woman's honor in court. Let me think about it. My brothers worry much about *my* honor, and I do not think they would like it if you spoke as rudely to *them* about their ethics."

He said he'd be proud to come back later. But she wrote an address on her legal pad, tore the page off, and handed it to him saying, "I live alone, since both my brothers have been married. But come well after dark, discreetly, and if I do not answer to your first knock, go away. It will mean I have company."

He assured her he'd come calling on Mex ladies before, as he folded the paper and put it away. Then he said, "One more honest answer, and try hard. What might Gomez be to you and your firm, speaking of unethical lawyers?"

She shook her head and said, "Gomez is a common Spanish name. Pero an associate named Gomez in Nuevo Laredo? No. I thought you said he was working with la señorita's law firm, no?"

He nodded and got to his feet, saying, "He's supposed to be. I could tell you a tale of a dog that wasn't supposed to bite. But I can see you're anxious for me to leave. So I'll come by your place later and, speaking of unexpected bites, I feel it's only fair to warn you that when I get ambushed I tend to get mad as hell. I'm hoping we'll still be pals when all this is over."

She said she'd like that, too, if only someone would tell her what on earth was going on.

Chapter 5

Longarm didn't know how jealous Paddy O'Boyne
might be. But he figured it just as wise, and just as
truthful, to tell her he had to meet with a shady lawyer after dark, and that was how come he'd brought
home all the books, candy, and a pint of white rum in
case she got weary of reading. She said she understood his meeting-up with shady souls who might
know where that awful Perkins man was hiding out.
But she seemed to feel he owed her some adios slap-
and-tickle as well, and he was sorely tempted. For
she sure was a tempting little gal, even with her duds
on, and he wasn't figuring on getting more than information out of old Rosalinda. But as she rose from
the bed to wrap her naked charms about him he insisted, "You know how we both hate to stop once we
get started, and I ain't got time for a hot soak after-
wards."

Then he just had to say, "Speaking of hot soaks,
no offense, it might not be a bad idea for you to, ah,
wash up a mite in my absence."

It worked. She flared, "Are you saying I stink,
you dirty old man?"

To which he replied, truthfully enough, "Not
hardly. But it's been a spell, and you have done your
share of sweating, and there might not be time to

bath before we have to catch a train, if I come back with old T.J."

She snapped, "It would serve you right if I kissed him all over, you mean-talking thing. Get out of my sight, and, oh, tell the chica downstairs that I want some hot water up here, on the quick march! I'll show you who and what needs washing, you stinky old brute!"

He tried to kiss her. She turned her cheek to him. So he knew it was safe to leave and hoped she'd feel inspired by those love stories he'd bought for her. He couldn't get through such a book himself. The gals who wrote 'em sure had odd notions about men. He'd often wondered if that was what made spinster gals who read a lot so odd. Lover gents they met up with in those books just didn't act possible, let alone natural. The gals who wrote about it instead of getting to it seemed to figure they could find a man who talked and acted masterful as hell until he wound up alone with a gal, after which he was supposed to turn into a quivering lapdog who obeyed every command, some of 'em sort of peculiar.

He left the posada while it was still light, knowing how hard it was to set up an ambush or even get gents with prices on their heads out of doors.

The address Rosalinda had written down for him was a good walk, and he was mildly surprised to find she lived in a respectable part of town as well. Knowing she likely hadn't left her office in worse parts yet, Longarm strode down the far side bold as brass to get the whole layout of her block in mind. Farther down there was a little church. It was open, naturally. But he only stepped inside as far as the holy-water font. There was nobody watching the spiral stairs running up to the bell tower. So he went up them unseen as well as uninvited while, somewhere down below, a handful of sweet-voiced kids started singing. Vesper services were fixing to start, most likely.

Once he was up among the bells, which weren't much bigger than fire bells, he peered out and down to see that sure enough he had a bird's-eye view of the whole neighborhood. There was pigeon shit all over the windowsills to prove that.

He counted red-tile rooftops until he had Rosalinda's abode pinned down. The house was wrapped around a tree-shaded patio. It was old, but bigger than he'd expected. She'd said her parents had sent all their kids to college. If she was living alone in the family home her family had come down in the world a mite, if only socially. She'd as much as admitted the one elder brother had a drinking problem. It hardly mattered what bad habits she and the younger son might or might not have. Elder brothers ran things once their father was gone. The present head of Robles, Robles y Robles was running things into the ground. Caleb Woodward had sure picked a peach of a Mex law firm. But, of course, if you wanted to flimflam a neighbor lady you'd hardly pick decent lawyers to lie to her in writing.

After he'd been up there long enough to get mighty tired of pigeon shit, he spotted Rosalinda getting out of a hired hack in front of her place. She went in alone. He hadn't spotted movement on the street or on her patio, either. But, then, you weren't supposed to when a gunslick knew his business, and her business not only allowed but called for meeting up with many a sneaky cuss.

A pigeon came fluttering at him across the roof-tops, landed on the ledge below the opening he was peering from, and cocked its head to give him a suspicious beady-eyed once-over. Longarm muttered, "Howdy, bird. I wish I had wings right now. For if I did I might be able to sneak a look-see down into that gal's patio before I pounded like a trusting fool on her front door."

The pigeon offered no helpful comments. So Longarm studied in silence until he had the layout down yonder mapped in his head. It was almost dark enough to pay a call on a spinster lady, now. So as more fool birds fluttered in to bed down among the bells, he moved over to the head of the spiral staircase and eased down the now sort of gloomy shaft.

When he came out of the slot at the bottom Longarm found himself face to face with an old iron-haired gent in a long black priestly robe. Longarm nodded a howdy and headed on out. It didn't work. The priest said, softly but firmly, "I believe you owe me an explanation, señor."

Longarm had to agree that sounded fair. So he nodded and got out his badge and I.D., saying, "I presumed to take advantage of your bell tower as a lookout, Padre. You have my word I'm not a pigeon thief."

The old priest smiled despite himself and replied, "I never said you were. But, forgive me, I find it most mysterious that a peace officer would come all the way from Los Estados Unidos del Norte for to hunt *ladrones* in *this* parish. I am not at liberty to repeat the small sins I hear in my confessional, but I can tell you this is not the part of our great city in which to seek dangerous criminals."

73

He shot a disapproving glance at the gun grips peeking out at him from under Longarm's coat and added, "I take it your own government did not send you down here to arrest any other kind of criminal?"

Longarm smiled and said truthfully, "I doubt my government knows where I am right now. I was invited by your government to pick up a yanqui neither country has much use for. He got loose and headed deeper into Mexico. So here I am and your guess is as good as mine whether he's hid out here, there, or anywhere."

The priest prissed his lips and said they'd better talk some more about that. As he led Longarm through some mysterious passages he repeated this was hardly the part of Mexico City to hunt down desperados, Mex or Anglo, and hinted Longarm had to be holding out on him, if he wasn't fibbing outright.

So when they wound up in the old man's quarters, and Longarm found himself holding a wine glass with permission to smoke, he leaned back in the comfortable chair he'd been offered and told the firmly polite old priest, "I can see how your faith gets folk to confess. You don't give a body much choice. I'm not trying to confuse you, Padre. It's just that it's a mighty confusing case and I'd be wasting your time if I tried to go into it with you in detail."

The priest sat down across from Longarm as if he meant to stay a spell and said, "I have plenty of time. Try me."

So, seeing it was still early, Longarm told the older man the whole story, starting at the border and leaving out some dirty parts. He didn't know whether Paddy was Roman Catholic for sure, and if she was she could do her own confessing, if she wanted.

Longarm didn't offer the name of the other lady he knew in the neighborhood. Rosalinda could do her own confessing as well. The old priest accepted the simple fact that Longarm had an after-dark call to pay on someone who might or might not be able to give him a line on where a shady gringo might find it easy to hide out in Mexico City. For a man who said his parishioners didn't confess all that much, Padre Filipe, as he called himself, had a pretty good grasp on the owlhoot trail. He poured more wine for the both of them and said, "I doubt your man is hiding among the poor and desperate of our sprawling slums. I mean no insult to your people, but it is a simple fact that all too many of our lower classes simply hate el gringo. This Perkins you seek would be welcomed like a long-lost brother by many who might secretly hate him, as long as his money held out. For every lowlife with a room or a daughter for rent, there must be many more who could only hope to profit by turning him in. La policia pay informers well under our current form of government. I would not seek this Perkins among the known haunts of our own criminal class if I were you. He had, how you say, nothing going for him there, eh?"

Longarm nodded thoughtfully and decided, "I doubt a Mexican bandit could hide out long in Clay County, Missouri, no matter how the folk there feel about old Frank and Jesse James. Perkins is said to be a jewel thief when he ain't killing lawmen, come to study on it. You don't see many jewels worth stealing in a slum. The one time I met him he was dressed Anglo cow, but he'd been picked up trying to sneak into Texas. I don't know how good his

75

Spanish might be. But he's got black hair, and lots of Mexicans of pure Spanish blood are blue-eyed blonds when you study on it. So a man who dressed right and talked right could be living as respectable as he might want to, high above the huddled masses."

Longarm took another sip of wine and added, "I wish I hadn't said that. Mexico City is way bigger than Denver, and I wouldn't know where to begin in Denver if my want could be holed up in *any* infernal part of town."

Longarm put the glass down and got up from the chair, saying, "I doubt I'll catch Perkins lighting a candle out front, no offense. So I'd best be on my way, Padre."

The old priest rose to show him out. Along the way he softly asked, "Would you be willing to take the poor sinner alive, or do you prefer your wanted killers neatly boxed, my son?"

"I consider it more professional to bring 'em back alive, Padre. The choice is up to them. Why do you ask?"

Padre Filipe softly replied, "The poor sinner may be desperate, and Mother Church has eyes and ears in every part of Mexico. It may strike you as silly, but if there was some way to arrange a peaceful surrender—"

"I doubt Perkins would go for it," Longarm cut in. "Your mother is free to try, and I, for one, would feel mighty obliged. But we're not talking about a wayward youth, Padre. Timothy James Perkins is a man full grown and a full-blown killer as well. He knows that no matter how gentle I treat him he'll still wind up with a rope around his neck if there's any justice at all. I wouldn't be chasing him so persistent if he hadn't killed so many mild-mannered arresting officers."

The old man looked so sad and wistful that as they got to the steps out front Longarm felt obliged to assure him, "Feel free to try, though, Padre. If your fellow sky pilots can locate the rascal and talk him into giving up, you have my word I won't harm a hair on his head, unless he makes me."

The priest asked Longarm to stop by again in a day or so. They shook on it and parted friendly, the old man going back inside and Longarm striding into the cool shades of evening to see if he could come up with something more sensible.

It was now about as dark as it figured on getting, since the almanac promised a full moon would be above the rooftops any minute now. Longarm turned away from the direction of Rosalinda Robles's street entrance. He liked to know what he might be entering in a strange neighborhood after dark. He circled around to the alley running along the spine of her city block. The telegraph or telephone poles he'd spotted from the church tower still ran along the alley. He didn't care whether the cable company had taken a shortcut across town or whether this part of the city had gotten high toned to the point of using Bell's new contraptions. Either kind of pole could be climbed as well.

So a short time later, as Rosalinda Robles was enjoying a cool-off in the usually total privacy of her patio, she let out a holler and jumped out of her big garden fountain to streak for the nearest cover as Longarm dropped down from the roof tiles to land lightly as he could in the shrubbery on that side. His unexpected vertical entrance had cut the naked lady off from the bedroom where her evening wear lay waiting, so she wound up playing Eve in the Garden of Eden behind an oleander bush with her bare behind pressed to rough stucco. It wasn't near as big a bush as a gal her size needed to cover her charms total. Longarm ticked the brim of his Stetson at her and said, "Buenos noches. I hope I'm not too early."

The embarrassed señorita stammered, "You most certainly *are*! I was expecting you to knock, as most guests seem to manage! Do you always drop from the sky as ladies are freshening up after work?"

He smiled sheepishly and explained, "I wanted to make sure we were alone."

To which she replied, trying not to giggle, "We most certainly are and, unless you mean to dishonor me further, would you mind fetching me my robe, at least? You will find it on the bed, just inside that open French window behind you."

He nodded, ducked into a dark room scented with enough posies for a funeral parlor, and found a silk-brocaded house robe where she said he might. He carried it back out and headed for her oleander bush with it. She pleaded, "No closer, por favor. Just toss it over this silly little bush and be good enough to turn the other way por un momento."

He did as he was told. She sure sounded slithery as she got all those naked curves under cover with slick silk. He'd seen more than he felt he'd better mention as he'd peered down over the eaves of her roof after shinnying up that pole out back. It might have been stretching the truth to say she'd resembled a nymph splashing bare-assed in that fountain. The nymphs he'd seen in picture books seemed a mite skinnier. But the effect on his glands had been much

the same, and when she told him he could turn
round, he hardly found the effect all that calming.
The soft light of the patio lamps shone on the shiny
silk robe in a way to leave little to the imagination
and, having seen her before she'd put it on, he didn't
have to imagine all that much. She sure had a skinny
waist when one considered how she bulged above
and below it. She must have sensed what he was
staring at so politely. She blushed and said, "Well,
since we seem to have no secrets from each other,
would you like a drink? I know I could use one right
now!"

He followed her inside. It was just his luck she led
him into a damned old parlor with a sofa facing a
cold fireplace. She sat him there and moved over to a
monsterous oak sideboard to build them some mon-
strous drinks. She'd offered passion-flower juice at
her office. As he tasted the tall order she handed
him, he saw she drank more serious off duty. It tasted
like white rum, a heap of white rum, with maybe a
dab of sloe gin or perfume mixed in to make serious
drinking seem more refined.

She plopped herself down beside him, as if unaware a gal built like that needed more than a waist
sash to hold such a robe closed down her front
enough to matter. He suspected, since there'd been a
dress and underthings across that bedspread as well,
that she figured since the damage had been done
there was little point in trying to persuade a gentle-
man caller that she had no tits. She inhaled at least a
quarter of her drink before she regarded him archly
over the rim of her glass to say, "I think I understand
why you dove into the patio from the roof instead of
knocking. You feared I might be a bad girl, no?"

He swallowed his own politer sip and said, "I wasn't worried about you being bad, personal. B one time in Sonara a señorita invited me to a la supper as turned out to be more like a shoot-out. I can see now that you'd never set a poor wandering gringo up that way, but it's better to be safe than sorry. I did tell you I was searching for a killer who may run in a pack, you know."

She nodded and said, "Is early for to discuss how safe I am, you wicked caballero. Had you come in the proper way, allowing me to receive you more properly, I was prepared for to tell you I have put out, how you say, feelers? Neither of my brothers could recall the name of this Perkins. Pero one doubts he would use his right name if he was hiding out in the Mexican underworld. I have learned of a mysterious gringo answering to the name of Teem. Is the first letter of T. J. Perkins, no?"

He nodded and said, "Timothy James is what the T. J. stands for. I can see why he'd as soon be known as T. J. I used to get teased about Custis. Teem would be the way your folk might pronounce it. So how do I go about meeting up with this mysterious Teem?"

She shrugged, unaware of what that did to the already low vee of her gown, as she told him, "Nada. He is not at the posada where he was staying with a woman of low repute. She is most cross with him for deserting her without a word of explanation. That is how I happen to have heard the gossip. Her pimp is looking for this Teem, too. It seems he owes money for services rendered."

Longarm nodded, sipped more liquid fire, and de- cided, "That means that whether it was Perkins or

not, he won't be showing his face in that part of town
___ if he's got a lick of sense. I was just talking to
___ old gent about the odds on a wanted gringo
___ out amid the more disreputable folk in this big
___ n. Perkins is slick to the point of sickening. It
would be just like him to drag a red herring through
parts of this town I might not be safe in myself."

She finished her drink and got up to pour herself
another as she asked, apparently still sober, "What is
this red herring thing you mention? I fear my grasp
of your language is limited."

As she rejoined him, plopping down a mite more
heavily this time, he explained, "Let's not worry
about U.S. slang. This mysterious Teem could be
just what he sounds like, a no-good drifter who's
going to wind up facedown in some alley at the rate
he's going. An international crook like Perkins would
know better than to run out on a shady lady, owing
money, unless he wanted it to get around, as it did,
that he or someone that could be him had crawled
into the worse parts of the city just so we'd keep
looking for him there. His yellow sheets, I mean
criminal record, hint he's spent lots of time in Mexico and Central America. He'd know the customs. If
his Spanish is good enough he could likely get by as
a respectable Mex when he wasn't out to leave false
scents. So I thank you for the tip, but I doubt it
would be worth following up on, now that he's run
off on the gal he was shacked up with, in any case."

She sighed and said, "I have other people asking
about for his whereabouts."

"I have another gent in this same neighborhood
doing the same. I mean to keep in touch with both of

you. Lord knows I've no notion where else to search for the rascal."

She nodded soberly, considering, and told "You shall find me ready to receive you here evening after working hours. I do not think y should try to contact me again at the office. My olde brother got most excited when he heard from the palm reader on the second landing that we had had a gringo calling on us. I explained you meant us no harm and that you were not connected with our own policia. Pero he has this problem and it makes him so suspicious and short-tempered at times."

Longarm muttered dryly, "I've heard such problems tend to run in families. Mum's the word."

He'd said it half to himself, without thinking, so he was caught by surprise when she suddenly flared, "And just who are you calling names?"

Then, before he could even try to answer, she'd buried her head in his chest to commence bawling like a baby. He took her in his arms to soothe her, as he asked her, "What in thunder did I say? It was you as intimated your brother was a drunk. I've never even met the cuss!"

She sobbed, "You said it was a family curse and called me a mum, whatever that means!"

So he held her closer to pat her silky back as he soothed, "I meant I wasn't going to bother you at your office. Mum means *silencio*, see?"

She sniffed and insisted, "Then for why did you say our whole family drank too much? My younger brother and me never drink during office hours. Is it wrong for to settle one's nerves after work with a little drink?"

He moved both their huge glasses safely out of the

way as he assured her, "There you go. You and me and your younger brother qualify as sensible drinkers 'stead of drunks. It ain't what you drink or even w much you drink when you do it sensible. Your ue drunk is one who drinks when most folk wouldn't, like on the job or getting ready for a meeting where a clear head might be called for. There ain't no harm in getting sloshed like this, when you're only being sociable with old friends."

She giggled in his arms and confided, "It does feel as if we have known one another longer than we have. Perhaps it is because you have seen me naked, no?"

He chuckled and said, "Well, that is a good way to break the ice, old pal. Meanwhile, it's getting sort of late, and you've told me what I came to hear, so I'd best be going while I'm still sober enough to let go of such a pretty little thing."

She hung on to him, asking why he had to leave so soon and did he really think she was little. She said, "I try for to keep my weight under control. But is hard for to resist nibbling perhaps too much, alone, when one lives so alone."

He shrugged and suggested it was up to her to find herself someone to keep her company after work. Rosalinda was a gal you just had to watch what you muttered at. For the next thing he knew she was all over him, the robe open total, now, as she smothered him with kisses and groped at his own duds.

He didn't want to have to explain busted fly buttons to Paddy, if and when he ever got back to their posada. So in order to protect his duds he felt obliged to take them off. Then they wound up on the rug together, acting mighty friendly for quite a spell.

There was much to be said for a well-padd _him,_
riere on a rug with tiles set under it. He on _any_
worry about bruising his own knees as old _you_
did most of the work. Longarm was a big
every way, as she exclaimed with delight.   she
had him bouncing like a baby on her knee,   ould
have, had she had him on her knees instead of between 'em. He enjoyed the way the rest of her felt.
Any man would have. But even as he was coming in
her he felt sort of chagrined to find himself in such a
dumb situation.

From the way she was carrying on as she kissed
and screwed him silly she seemed to think she'd
found her prince charming at last, for keeps. Gals
could be like that. Their big brothers could take it
even more serious if you left 'em feeling used and
abused. So even when they wound up back on the
sofa in an even more interesting position, his brain
was mighty vexed with his less thoughtful parts as it
considered the cold gray dawn, whatever the hell
time it was right now.

She solved a heap of explaining he was trying to
come up with when, without warning, she simply
stopped bouncing and commenced to snore. Two tall
glasses of white rum could have that effect on anybody. Since he hadn't had nearly that much himself,
Longarm was able to dismount quietly without disturbing her sated and unconscious charms. He got
dressed again as he considered his next move. He
considered leaving a note. But as he strapped his gun
back on he decided his best move would be to turn
back into a frog and get out, pronto. There was no
telling who might read a note before she ever woke

again, and there was no nice way to write such an adios in any case.

He eased out into the patio and headed for the ̲ular way out. Then he spied a passion-flower vine ̲wing up to the roof and decided there was no ̲ense shocking any neighbors who might be nosy about such a wild young gal living alone on their street. He climbed the vine, slipped across the roo̲ tiles the way he'd come before, and dropped int̲ back alley to take off in the darkness.

So he never heard the conversation in a door niche a pistol-shot from Rosalinda's front door. A surly voice muttered in English, "What could be keeping him in there all this time? Do you reckon he's fixing to spend the night with her, T.J.?" To which his companion replied with an evil grin, "Wouldn't you if you could, Geek? It's early yet. What goes in has to come out, sooner or later. So hold your horses and give the son of a bitch time to set himself up right for us."

Chapter 6

The evening was in fact still young and Longarm
wasn't about to bed with another woman before he'd
given his back a rest and taken in some more liquids.
He had to pass through downtown Mexico City getting from Rosalinda's fancier neighborhood to that
posada near the railyards. So he walked slow, keeping an eye out for a sidewalk cantina that might still
be serving cerveza and sit-downs.

He knew there'd be plenty. Mexicans tended to be
night-folk, and those who didn't have private patios
tended to live in the street until way past midnight.

As he approached the brighter lights of the less-
sedate parts of town he saw some of them were paper
lanterns. They had so many fool fiestas down this
way that he'd often wondered why they took the lanterns down between times. An old woman dozing on
her bare heels against a wall had a basket of white
candy skulls next to her as she waited with Apache
patience for business to pick up in the morning. The
sugar frosting and licorice skulls she'd no doubt
baked at home likely meant they were fixing to hold
the odd fiesta called The Day of Death. It was sort of
like Halloween only more so. Spanish-speaking folk
seemed to have more fun with the grim reaper than
Victorian folk farther north thought proper.

He found a neighborhood shop open, lit up by

hissing gas jets, that sold candied cockroaches, real ones, fake skulls and bones of cake topping and, better yet, cold cerveza in bottles. There was no place to sit down, but the suds wet his whistle fine as he strode on with a cold brown bottle in each fist. Nobody he passed seemed to care. The notion one could get away with drinking on the street by keeping the bottle in a brown paper bag was a pure yanqui tion. You paid extra for bags in Mexico when didn't carry along your own string shopping bag.

By the time he'd drained both bottles he'd covered some ground and there was the blue and white sign of the cable company near the main plaza where it was supposed to be. So he ambled in to wire his current where and why to his home office. It didn't take him long to block out his message, since Billy Vail had no need to know about either Paddy or Rosalinda, and he was damned if he knew where T. J. Perkins might be right now.

As he handed it over, the young gal at the counter had to read it, if only to see where to send it. She asked what a few of the English words might mean. He told her she looked a mite too young and she fluttered her lashes and allowed that was what she thought they might mean. Then she told him there was a message for him if he was really U.S. Deputy Custis Long. He was mildly surprised to see Billy Vail had guessed where he'd headed after Nuevo Laredo and even more surprised at the bulk of Billy's message. For even at night-letter rates, old Billy just hated to spend money needlessly.

Longarm thanked the pretty telegraph clerk and put the tome in a side pocket to read sitting down. He found a place to do that just across the plaza, if he was reading Spanish at all correctly. But as he was crossing the wide-open space a spooky little gal of twelve or thirteen took his left hand in her own grubby little paw to say, "If you wish for to give me a centavo I wish for to be your friend."

It wasn't a kid being out that late on a Mexican street that spooked him. It wasn't her implied offer that spooked him. They had to start sometime and some gents liked 'em young. It was the papier-maché skull she had on over her head that he found a mite unsettling. He said politely, "I might give you a centavo if you promise not to tell your little friends. You'd better grow some before we talk about *how* friendly you may be."

She laughed—it sounded mighty strange to hear a young girl laughing inside even a fake skull—and told him, "Do not say bad things about me. I am still a virgin, almost. Give me the centavo and I will tell you something I do not think you know."

That sounded fair. Even if she called him a dumb gringo and ran off laughing he'd still come out ahead. So he reached his other hand in a pocket and handed her the smallest coin he could come up with. She held it up to the ominous eye socket of her odd headware and said, "Oh, muchas gracias, señor! Nobody has ever given me cinco centavos before!"

He muttered, "I'm sure you'll get there. What do I get for my hard-earned Mexican nickel? *No tengo mas.*"

She gripped his hand tighter and said, "You are being followed by two other hombres, both gringo, like yourself. They have been following you since you came out of the telegrafo. I thought you might

88

like to know. What kind of trouble might you be in, eh?"

Without breaking stride he muttered, "It'll cost a centavo to find out. Otherwise, just run along and play. Let them think you just begged a coin and let all us grown-ups forget all about you."

The streetwise waif didn't have to be told twice. She ran off to pester other strollers as Longarm strode on across to the cantina and swung around naturally as he helped himself to a wire seat at an empty tin table. He saw at once that he'd gotten his money's worth. He might not have noticed two gents dressed yanqui in suits and ties amid the other strollers if he hadn't been warned to watch for 'em. Now that he had, he couldn't help noticing how both their suits bulged. As he gave a sleepy-eyed waiter his order Longarm casually drew his side arm so he could cover them, under the table. They both kept coming, striding in step, until they were as close as he wanted them to be, and he called out conversationally, "Halt, and don't bank on me saying that three times. I hate to be the one who has to tell you this, boys, but I got the drop on you."

The one to Longarm's left said, "We assumed you might, Long. Hold your damned fire. I'm Agent Wallace, U.S. Secret Service, and this is my pard, Fitzroy. We expected you might turn up at the cable office. But you sure dart out of places for a man your size. We didn't think it advisable to shout at you from behind on a strange street in a strange town after dark."

Longarm nodded and said, "Don't ever do that by broad day, if you don't dodge good. I'd like to see some I.D. Anyone can say they're anything, and I don't see any business I might have with Treasury. I ride for Justice, myself."

As both secret service agents gingerly drew their leather billfolds to flash their bitty gold badge him, Wallace told him, "That's what we wanted talk to you about. We're down here working out the U.S. Consulate. It's our job to keep an eye on other Yanks who could be drifting into trouble. What kind of trouble are you fixing to cause this time, Longarm?"

Their friendly rival chuckled and invited them to join him for some liquid refreshment before he confided, "I ain't here to overthrow the government. Plenty of decent Mexicans are fixing to do that as soon as they get the chance. I'm down here to pick up a want called T. J. Perkins. He's the sort of Americano you don't want running loose in *any* country."

The two agents ordered the same as the waiter returned with Longarm's tall drink. Fitzroy said, "We know about Perkins. He's on *our* shit-list, or he was. We'd heard he'd been nabbed near the border and that someone from your department was coming to pick him up."

"Ancient history," Longarm said, and proceeded to fill his fellow lawmen in as the three of them sipped gin and tonic. As he wound down, Longarm got out the long telegram from Billy Vail, adding, "Stay put a spell while we find out if my boss has been paper trailing again. Old Billy Vail got fat hunting owlhoots with the help of the post office and Western Union. But I have to allow he's a wonder at it."

He tore open the tome and held it to the dim light

to scan as Wallace ordered another round. The drinks arrived before Longarm got to the end. But not by much. He put the long message away, picked up his s, and said, "I'm sure glad you boys didn't head way *after* I'd read all that. Perkins, as I hope you now, is a killer who moves faster than reasonable. The Texas Rangers report two of his known associates crossed the border recent at El Paso–Juarez. The Rangers had no call to stop either. They'd done nothing since last they got out of prison. We can forget the one called Lobo Logan. He's described as a clubfoot with vulpine features. He met with a fatal accident up in Monterrey the other day. I didn't spot the jasper the Rangers say Logan went to Juarez with and never came back. He describes mighty average and he's called Geek Grogan. His yellow sheets read he ran off with a circus as a teenaged town thief. I reckon they call him Geek because, having no other circus talents, he worked as a wild man from Borneo at first, biting heads off chickens and eating rats alive. His real name's Mervin Grogan. I can see why he'd just as soon be called Geek."

He wet his whistle some more and continued, "He graduated to midway barker, then left the circus after fighting over some freak-show gal and winning beyond reason. He drew twelve-at-hard for manslaughter, with time off for good behavior. His cellmate for a good part of that time was T. J. Perkins. Need I say more?"

Wallace shook his head to agree, "Birds of a feather sneak together. If Perkins sent for extra killers to join him down here, would you say that meant he aimed to go back peaceable?"

Longarm shrugged and replied, "I doubt he was

planning on returning to the states at all. He was picked up on this side of the border, holed up with other scum of the female persuasion, or so he said. He could have been in that border town for any di business I can think of. He steals, he robs, he smu gles, and if you don't watch out, he kills. I'd say h was there to greet yet another old pal he'd sent for."

Fitzroy asked, "Why couldn't he have been fixing to smuggle something when the Mex law tripped over him?"

To which Longarm replied with a weary look, "If he'd had an undeclared clay piggy bank on him los rurales would have found it. They don't just strip-search a gringo they catch up with in a whorehouse. They tear the whorehouse up while they're at it, and the whores know better than to hold out on los rurales if they want to get off with no more than a few bruises."

He sipped at his glass thoughtfully, then said, "Hold on. He did say something about buried treasure he'd share with me if the two of us busted out. Los rurales had me locked in with him 'til they were paid off. But, hell, Perkins knew I was there to claim a known jewel thief and I knew he was out to flimflam me just to get him out of there alive. If he did have anything he'd hidden in or near Nuevo Laredo, it's long gone by now. The slippery son of a bitch left town on a train and a good many hours ahead of me."

"Then what makes you so sure he's hiding out here in Ciudad Mejico?" Fitzroy asked. "It's a big country, you know, and he has to know you're after him."

"Make that *us*," Wallace said. "The political situa-

tion is sort of delicate right now, with Diaz about to
stage one of his fake elections, and the last thing we
need is another big jewel robbery and everyone dash-
ing about with drawn guns!"

Longarm waved the waiter in for another round as
he said, "Tell me about the last one. All I had on
Perkins was that he was wanted in the states for a lot
of hell-raising. How much hell has he raised on your
beat, boys?"

Wallace growled, "Do we look like the god-
damned Policia de Mejico? Our job is to guard the
staff at the consulate and see what we can do for
honest American travelers. Neither is half as easy as
we'd like it."

Longarm frowned and pointed out, "It was Treasury agents the cuss just murdered in New Orleans,
you know."

"Customs men, not Secret Service, and does this
look like New Orleans?"

Fitzroy soothed, "It ain't that we're not at all interested. The Mex law just doesn't invite us to go
through their files that often. As we put it together,
Perkins robbed a licensed jeweler and receiver of
stolen goods, close to a million's worth of first water
or top-grade diamonds. The kind that's hardest to
I.D. and handiest to unload without no settings."

Longarm whistled softly and asked, "Is it safe to
assume the victim had a government license to fence
stolen goods as well?"

So both Treasury men laughed as one. It was Wallace who pointed out that the Mex law even took a
rake-off from the stalls in the thieves' market that
wasn't supposed to exist in the old town between the
cathedral and railroad yards. Fitzroy said, "The rob-

93

bery never happened, on paper. But we figure Perkins still has about half of the booty left. It was a spell back and it costs mucho dinero to hide out down here with the so-called law out to catch up with you at any price. Perkins lost almost a quarter-m̶ when he tried to sneak through Customs at New C̶ leans. We don't know how our boys spotted that false bottom in his steamer trunk. He left 'em in no condition to say. But he had to leave trunk and contents when he departed sudden in a blaze of glory. The New Orleans copper badges who wanted to talk to him about coming down the gangplank so noisy were lucky as he was, in all that gunsmoke, and by the time it cleared he was gone. The rest you know."

Longarm shook his head and insisted, "Not by half. I didn't even know he'd come in by ship until just now. My warrant just said he was wanted for a heap of crimes, with that one glossed over as just another murder charge. Where would he have hopped a ship at this end, Vera Cruz?"

Wallace shrugged and said, "That was the steamer's port of call. You can't hardly catch any seagoing vessel up here in Mexico City. But Vera Cruz is a short enough train ride."

Fitzroy nodded eagerly and said, "That's where I'd hunt for old T.J. if I was you, Longarm. He's hot as a whore's pillow here in the capital and we could really use more sleep."

Wallace explained, "Mex politics is already tense enough right now. El Presidente feels insulted by all the things businessmen up north have been saying about his notions of democracia. So we figure he means to match our next election by staging one against a puppet of his choice. It won't really matter if the votes are tallied honest, just this once. But he don't want *too* many votes cast against him, lest it seem odd when he stays on to run things in some other appointed capacity. In sum, he's got los federales, los rurales and la policia watching everyone like hawk⸎ ⸎th instructions to nip any and all arguments i⸎ ⸎by gunning any and all unfortunates argu-⸎ ⸎er side, about most anything. We've been trying to ease our own citizens out of the country 'til things simmer down again. But will they listen? So how do you feel about Vera Cruz? Nobody pays much attention to noise in Vera Cruz. Tough little seaports are like that."

Longarm finished his drink, decided he'd had enough, and told them, "I'd be proud to chase Perkins to Vera Cruz if I had any indication he might be there. At least one of his known associates fell down and busted himself en route to Mexico City. I've had one report, since, of a mysterious gringo messing up in the shady parts of town no decent gringo has any business hanging out in. So I'll keep Vera Cruz on the back of the stove for now. He'd be dumb to hop another steamer now that he's seen how picky U.S. Customs can be, next to miles and miles of wide-open border any jackrabbit can cross with a modest amount of common-sense caution."

Wallace objected, "He got caught near the border at Nuevo Laredo, didn't he? Leave us not forget that was *after* he was spotted arriving by sea."

Longarm got to his feet, saying, "I don't think he was meaning to cross into Texas there. He knows he's famous. So why would he want to risk hanging, in more places than one, when we know he has pals less well-known who'd be able to smuggle the rest of

95

his hot ice, if that's what he's really up to? Geek Grogan describes just tedious and don't have nearly as long a record. There's no wanted paper on the polecat since he finished his time and they had to turn him loose."

Fitzroy objected, "You just established him as a killer."

But Longarm just shrugged and said, "He's got to kill again before I can even turn him over my knee for a good spanking. Try her this way. Perkins was waiting in that border town for his old cellmate. He meant to hand something to Grogan, after which a gent the border guards had just seen crossing over for some cactus candy would have drifted back, packing, say, one of them straw vaqueros or a genuine Mexican flowerpot, to deliver the stolen diamonds to most any fence in the U.S. of A."

Longarm dropped some coins on the table and added, "It went wrong. Los rurales picked Perkins up as he waited. Not wanting to be sent back here, he confessed he was wanted in the states, and then things got even more confusing when others butted in for their own reasons. I figure Perkins streaked back here to hide out some more and give things a chance to cool down. Since his pal, Grogan, never returned to Texas with his straw vaquero, I figure he's followed Perkins and, right about now, the whole bunch is cooking up something else. I'm glad you boys told me about the uneasy political situation here. That explains the usually lazy rurales jumping a casual cathouse visitor and— Thunderation! It *works*!"

Both Secret Service men demanded he do better than that. So he confided, "I sort of discounted rumors of a mysterious Anglo called Teem, or Tim, or T.J., messing up with some Mex pimp by treating a puta unfair. If Perkins behaved as such an inexperienced traveler in a Nuevo Laredo house of ill repute, it's small wonder he got grabbed by los rurales. They get a cut on all the border-town vice in every border town. I've been playing chess when the game's just checkers, again. I've been picturing Perkins as a slick crook instead of the asshole he must really be! It's been swell talking to you gents. Now I'd best get cracking."

Back at the posada, Paddy O'Boyne insisted it was way too late to do anything but screw, and added that he'd been drinking. He assured her, "Just rum, beer, and gin, honey. I never drink much when forced to mix social drinking. I don't mean to prowl the *garito* parts of town before we have you safely aboard a northbound to Santa Fe. But there's one pulling out around midnight. So if you'd like to get dressed . . ."

She sat bolt upright in bed, allowing the sheet to fall down the swell front of her, as she protested, "You can't abandon me like this, Custis!"

"Not like that, for sure. You'd best pin your hair up and cover it with that black lace as well. I've damn-it *done* what I could for you, Paddy. The whole trip was a dumb practical joke or a ruse. Your old Spanish grant is the real thing and rock solid. Nobody can take your land. It's time you got back to keep an eye on your cows. You ought to know by now how much I enjoy your company. But to tell the truth you're slowing me down a heap. I wouldn't have had to come all the way back here if I only had my fool self to consider, so . . ."

She started shaking with sobs in a way that

tempted him to touch her as well, all over. She protested, "I dasn't go all the way home alone! What if that mean Caleb Woodward has me done in by one of his henchmen?"

"The one with the foxy face and funny walk was a pal of T. J. Perkins, the man I'm after."

But she insisted, "Then why was he trailing *me*, in El Paso?"

It was a good question. He mused aloud, "I'll be switched with snakes if I see how a thief and killer with a hair-trigger temper and little else going for him could be tied in with a big cattle man, unless I'm missing something."

He'd already shucked everything but his pants and boots, sort of thoughtlessly while he had so much else on his mind. So he sat on the bed beside her to grunt off his boots as he mused, half to himself, "The old shell game looks mighty dumb at first glance. Anyone can see where the infernal pea ought to be and, even if you're wrong, the odds should still be one out of three, but—"

She wrapped her arms around him from behind to press her naked breasts to his bare back as she demanded, "Put yourself in my shell, you big tease."

So he did. It was relaxing to know where some things really fit together. He'd recovered amazingly from his similar experience with old Rosalinda earlier that night. It was likely because the two gals were so dissimilar.

Aside from not being built alike, they didn't move their hips at all alike, albeit both moved mighty grand. As he moved in Paddy he wondered what it would be like to have 'em both in bed side by side, so a man could sort of play musical love-saddles as he tried to decide.

He doubted either would go for it. It sounded like more fun for the man in the middle of the sandwich than for either sweet slice. But, Lord have mercy, a man could likely kill himself with the fool notions he got about women if women were willing to go along with everything men thought up when they were feeling frisky.

Old Paddy had apparently had time, alone so long, to frisk herself up as well. She insisted he was moving too slow and made him let her get on top. He didn't mind. He had to allow she could post on his saddle horn full gallop with her strong horsewoman's seat. As she did, high and low, he judiciously considered the contrast between her swell innards and the way it had felt in another gal that same evening. It made him even harder. The soft plump Rosalinda had been built naturally tight, bless her, while this more athletic little thing could take all he had without that look of dismay and passionate gasps, while at the same time, she could grip him as tight or tighter with muscles he doubted Rosalinda had ever used. Paddy went at it horny as a man might have, and laughed wickedly when she felt him ejaculating in her, instead of moaning that she'd never meant to go that far on her poor late father's very rug as Rosalinda had. He felt sure he just loved them both as he held Paddy in his arms to soothe her through a long shuddering orgasm that made her giggle instead of cry. For, Lord bless 'em, they were both great little gals and it was too bad the three of them hadn't been born Turks or even Mormons.

As they shared a smoke, drifting back down to the

bed from where they'd been floating amid the pink clouds of passion, he knew she didn't want to hear where else he'd had it that evening, so he just told her not to fall asleep before he could get it up again. She took the matter in hand to stroke it tenderly as she giggled and said, "Goody. I never wanted to catch that old train, anyway."

He sighed and said, "I noticed. I ain't sure you ought to head home alone, either, as I study on the ways of dumb crooks. It's a plain fact that at least two pals of T. J. Perkins were spotted in and about El Paso. The rest of us met miles east at Nuevo Laredo. They might have tried to scare you into crossing there instead of Juarez, just so you could get mixed up with me. They'd have known I was headed there to pick their pal up and—"

"Custis Long!" she cut in, gripping his poor privates as if she was afraid he'd buck her out of bed. "I'll have you know I heard of that nasty Perkins before *I* bailed him out, just to get to meet you and tag along with you! Are you trying to make me out a false-hearted woman, out to do you dirty?"

He hauled her top parts closer and kissed the part of her hair, soothing with his tone but stating plain facts as he told her, "It's happened. So far I've been luckier than poor old Sampson was in the Good Book. You'd be surprised how some gals have treated me after I'd gotten nice and dirty with 'em."

She wet his bare chest with tear drops as she insisted, "I wouldn't! I couldn't! Not after all we've been to each other!"

It would have been rude to mention others who'd tried to shoot him in the back after treating him so friendly. He just patted her bare shoulder and said, "I never call anyone a liar until they lie to me. So try not to as we go over the way we met, and watch them nails. There's some pieces of the puzzle we'd best examine calm and collected. It seems every time I try to talk calm to you it makes you want to excite me. But pay attention, just this once, hear?"

She stopped stroking him, so he went on. "I can't say our meeting up has been at all unpleasant. But let's go back over that, anyway. I was tossed in a jail cell with Perkins, the very crook I'd come to collect, when the next thing I knew that oily border lawyer, Gomez, bailed us out and brought me to you. I don't want to go over old Spanish land grants again, I'm out to narrow down such distractions. You say you got spooked at the El Paso–Juarez crossing and decided to cross at Laredo–Nuevo Laredo. You say you'd never heard of Perkins. Where did I come in?"

She replied soberly, "I'd heard of you, of course. Who hasn't heard of such a famous manhunter? But I didn't know you were in town, let alone the rurale lockup, before Señor Gomez told me. My law firm back home told me to look him up when I wired them I was afraid to meet their man in Juarez. By the time I got to Nuevo Laredo he'd taken care of all the railroad reservations and papers I might need. He'd booked me a suite at the best hotel near the hall of records and so forth. But he said he was afraid for my safety if I went on alone. He said things were in a stir down here and agreed those shabby men I'd spotted in El Paso could be agents of that mean Caleb Woodward."

Longarm took a drag on their cheroot and said, "He was right about things being even tenser than

101

usual down here right now. But I still don't see where I fit in."

"Oh, that was his idea, and you have to allow it worked out swell for me. He said if we could get you to go on down to the capital, owing me your freedom to do so, I'd be safe from just about anyone, as long as I was traveling with you."

She started stroking again as she added with a purr, "*This* part was my own inspired notion. Señor Gomez assured me you were a real gent with the ladies. I imagine he only knew you by reputation as well."

Longarm got rid of their cheroot as he mused aloud, "I mean to have a talk about that when next I meet that shady lawyer. He'd know better than me whether he was out to do me a hell of a favor or saddle me with excess baggage."

She sniffed and demanded to know just whom he was calling excess *baggage*.

He assured her he hadn't meant that the way General Howe and his redcoats had described the train of whores they'd drug along after old George Washington that time, but added, "You got to admit all them sweet young things slowed 'em down while our side was building a proper army and planning Howe's ruination. If I can't throw you to the mercy of a cow king's hired guns, and Lord knows how many other fresh gents, between here and your home spread, I'm still going to have to hole you up someplace safer and less out of the damned way. You say you already have a reservation at a decent hotel near the center of town?"

"Of course. I never planned on living so Mex

102

while I stayed here. But do you think that would be safe now?"

Longarm nodded and told her, "At least as safe as here, and a heap more comfortable. Even if Gomez told someone on the other side that you were staying at a regular hotel, by now they must have noticed you never arrived. I got Secret Service pals at the nearby U.S. Consulate. If you stay holed up, only sending out for room service now and again, while they stroll through the lobby now and again on their rounds—"

"Goody!" she cut in, "Only let's do it one more time before we have to get dressed and sneak across town in the dark!"

"Hold the thought. We got plenty of time and might even manage some sleep before broad day. Folk moving sneaky at night attract attention, even trying to look Mex as they creep up on fancy hotels late at night. They're holding an odd fiesta mañana. The Day of Death, with all the kids and half the adults dressed up like spooks. Come morning I'll duck out and fetch us some ghoulish masks and funeral shrouds. Then we'll just sort of haunt our way through the crowds until we get close enough to that hotel to slip in like a pair of lost souls, see?"

She didn't. The Day of Death wasn't all that popular among the Spanish folk of Santa Fe. Some local Aztec notions had apparently drifted in to what was just another Roman Catholic feast day anywhere else. But once she caught on she said she couldn't wait to dress up like a dead lady. Then she showed him how much life she had in her right now, as he groaned, "Hey, watch them *teeth*!"

Chapter 7

The Irish-American version of Halloween would no doubt seem a mite creepy to a visiting Chinaman. It was all in what one was used to. The Mexican Day of Death took some getting used to. Back home, kids dressed up as all sorts of things aside from ghosts. Down here there wasn't a fairy princess or pirate to be seen. Everyone was busting a gut trying to look as if they'd been dead a disgusting spell or, if they felt too sedate to act dead, they still had to dress as if they were at a funeral.

Nobody *acted* like they were at a funeral, of course. Everyone was smiling as they thronged the streets in family groups for the most part. Cheerful little kids dressed in black strolled with Mamacita and Papacito chewing on skull lollipops or downright gruesome parts of dead and decayed human bodies made of candy dyed to look like it had gangrene. Unmarried younger folk clowned and flirted as if a whole graveyard of long-dead sex maniacs had come back to life. It was hard to see what a green and pus-faced gent might see in a sweet young thing in a musty funeral shroud with her face painted or masked to look like a skull. But some were even kissing one another. It was a swell occasion for an otherwise prim and proper señorita to get goosed in public. Nobody that could tell her folk could be sure who the gooser was at any distance.

Paddy thought Longarm looked funny as hell with that big straw sombrero perched atop the papier-maché skull he had over his head, with a gray raggedy shroud hanging down to his boot tops so he could pack their two bags under it without looking more than grotesque. The shroud he'd picked out for her was musty black with streaks of graveyard earth painted on it. She insisted on tying the black lace shawl he'd bought here earlier under the chin of her own death's head. It didn't make her one lick prettier. The bloody bullet hole the mask maker had painted over her black left eye socket didn't make sense when you studied on it. But she sure looked awful.

Longarm left the serape-of-many-colors folded over the foot rail of the bed for the chambermaid and led his ghostly companion down to the street. Nobody noticed they were Americans, since they didn't even look human. They'd gone about two blocks when another lost soul pinched Paddy's bottom, heard the way she cussed him, and crawfished away, murmuring, "Sorry. I thought you were Maria."

She grabbed Longarm's left arm under their shrouds for comfort if not safety and her humor seemed restored when she spied some big odd-looking balloons bouncing along over the heads of the crowd and asked him, "Are those things what I think they are, Custis?"

He nodded his sombrero-topped skull and answered, "Yep. They were invented by a Dr. Condom around the time General Howe and his redcoats could have used 'em. They were made of sheep gut until

Goodyear figured out rubber back in the thirties. As you can see, Mex studs would rather blow 'em up to shock the señoritas than insult one by using as intended."

Paddy giggled and replied, "I told you I knew how to take care of myself without those dumb things in the way. But how come all the *colors*? I've never seen a green or purple condom before and, if I had, it might have scared me into second thoughts."

He chuckled and said, "The folk down here go in for colorful trimmings. I saw some condoms in a border-town shop made up to look like snakes, with eyes and a bitty rubber tongue, one time."

She laughed again and said, "Hmm, that tongue sounds sort of interesting, but *eyes*? I think we'd best stick to the way Adam and Eve started the whole thing, bless their horny souls."

He agreed he hated to take a bath with his socks on and led her through a shortcut to the plaza. A couple of decayed corpses were enjoying a wall job in the otherwise deserted arcade. Neither of them commented on such shocking behavior and the dead folk didn't stop. It wasn't too clear which one might be the he or she in any case.

He saw he might have made a tactical error when they found themselves haunting a nearly deserted side street. An old lady resting her elbows on a windowsill stared down at them with that thoughtful expression you see on lazy but mean yard dogs. At the next corner Longarm steered back to a crowded main street. The going was slower. But it felt safer, lost in a crowd of other walking dead. Paddy asked him to buy her a candy skull to eat. He growled, "They taste like sugared library paste, and don't you dare expose your gringo features at a time like this. We're getting there and you can send down for all the sweets you want after I have you safely hidden from folk that may take death more serious."

That was easier said than done. Foot traffic moved slow during any fiesta and The Day of Death was a humdinger. But at last he got Paddy to the hotel near the main plaza and the snooty room clerk acted as if graveyard corpses wandered in every day to ask for a corner suite with ajoining bath. He liked them even better when Longarm planted baggage on the floor and Paddy explained she had a reservation. The clerk dinged for a bellhop, handed over her key, and asked mildly, "La señorita from Nuevo Mejico is not traveling alone, as we were led to expect?"

Longarm said, inside his papier-maché skull, "That's all right. I'm just haunting her." So the clerk smiled down at the register and said he understood. So Paddy signed in and Longarm placed a silver dollar where he was supposed to sign, by Mex law. That seemed to be enough for the clerk.

The bellhop took them to the top floor in a fancy steam elevator and got a yanqui nickel for his trouble once the two visitors from the states were alone with their baggage. As Paddy peeled off her mock stare of death and decay, with a relieved woosh, Longarm said, "Bueno. Nobody here knows what you look like. Let's keep it that way. I see one of them new-fangled Bell telephones on the bedstand, yonder. Try not to overdo it as you call down for grub and such. Put that shawl on each time room service brings you something. That way, even should someone ask, you'll only be described as, sure, a yanqui lady and not bad-looking. I doubt anyone will risk taking an

107

axe to your door with only that to go on."

"Couldn't one of Caleb Woodward's hired guns just read the register I just signed, dear?"

"You had to sign in right to get this reservation. Hired guns ain't heavy readers, and anyone staked out downstairs last night will have reported you never showed. But you have a point. I'll take care of it on my way out."

She asked where and why he had to go out, unbuttoning the top of her bodice as she did so. He chuckled fondly and told her, "For God's sake, it ain't nearly noon yet and I'll never have a better chance to wander all over town disguised as a Mexican corpse. You just stay put here, and I'll get back to you when I get back to you. If I ain't back by bedtime, start without me. Like I said, it's time I got to move around without being tied to apron strings."

She asked him to at least kiss her good-bye. So he pulled off the paper skull and did so. Then, as long as he had it off, he went back down to the lobby packing his hat and extra head under his arm. But that didn't seem to spook the desk clerk either. Longarm placed the straw sombrero skull to one side on the marble countertop and hauled out his wallet to show the sophisticated Mex his badge and credentials. The clerk seemed mildly impressed. Longarm explained that he was on a mission both Mexico and the U.S. approved of and added, "La señorita upstairs is a material witness. I'd like to make sure she'll still be there when I get back. Has anyone else inquired about when or if she'd be staying here?"

The clerk shook his head to reply, "Pero no. And should anyone ask, we now know that an elderly widow named *Smeeth* occupies the room reserved for

La Señorita O'Boyne, who never arrived to verify her reservation . . ."

Longarm slapped another silver cartwheel down like a poker chip on the marble beside the hotel register. The clerk said, as he suavely tore out that page, "Our house detective shall have to be told. Once he has been alerted I fear for the safety of anyone trying to bother your, ah, witness. We run a first-class establishment here, catering to many important guests from your country. La policia understand why it is sometimes necesario to exterminate ratons discreetly, eh?"

They shook on it and Longarm put his papier-maché hat and straw sombrero back on, his real hat packed away with his possibles lest it wind up out of shape for good. He didn't spot the gent seated behind a copy of *La Prenza* in a corner chair. So as Longarm strode out the front entrance, looking spooky, the stakeout was already leaving via a side door near a clump of indoor jungle.

Longarm figured he'd fixed things with the hotel staff about as well as things could be fixed in a country run by ogres. Even ogres had some rules, and one of them was that useful visitors from el norte had to have some places where their lives and even their baggage would be safe. So the usually corrupt lawmen of the Diaz gang could go out of their way protecting folk in those few places off limits to gringo baiting.

Longarm chuckled inside the fake skull as he recalled the evening in Tijuana when he'd seen the way that worked at a fancy hotel he'd checked into with an even fancier gal. An older and fatter American lady staying there had picked up a good-looking Mex

109

young enough to be her grandson, and she'd no doubt been looking forward to raising him, up in her room, when a burly Mex detective stepped out from the rubber trees he'd been dozing in to tell the young slicker, "I reproach you for your stupidity. This is a four-star hotel." He'd then pistolwhipped the poor cuss to a state of downright ugly. The old gal who'd thought she was in for the screwing of her life calmed down a mite when they told her the Romeo of her dreams was a known jewel thief who just loved to flirt with rich old gals. The Mex police were too polite to say *she* was old and ugly, of course. They even found her a clean old man to help her through the night. So in the end she no doubt returned from her Mexican adventure singing the praises of El Presidente Diaz and his gallant lawmen.

But just in case he hadn't covered all bases, Longarm headed next for the nearby U.S. Consulate. The U.S. Secret Service hardly ever screwed fat old ladies to keep them from crying. But he hoped to get someone like Wallace or Fitzroy to drop in now and again to make sure Paddy was still safe and sound. The streets up that way were less crowded, since lost souls mostly haunted closer to home and the consulate was situated in a business area. As he swung the corner of the block the consulate was on, a couple of tiny ghosts were coming his way blowing whistles shaped like human bones. The brass door of the consulate ahead was solidly closed. But he doubted the U.S. government knocked off for Mexican spook days. Another spook of more adult size lounged in a closed storefront directly across from the consulate. That seemed fair until Longarm noticed the new boots shining from under the ragged cobweb-gray funeral shroud the cuss was wearing under his own death's head, painted a pale ghastly green. The ghost outfit was pure Mex. The boots were machine-stitched Justins, made in the USA. Longarm slowed down to study on that as he approached the oddly lonesome celebrant of a grim but gay fiesta. Mex gents wanting to look up-to-date were prone to spring for Saint Louis high-buttons, preferably polished yaller dog. Mex vaqueros wore boots along the line of Justins, since the gringo cowboy boot's design had been swiped from the same sources. But all cow-hands, north and south, prided themselves on their boots and liked to sport the best brand they could afford. Vaquero boots hand-stitched in Mexico were about as fancy as boots came, and not as expensive down here. So how come a gent dressed up other-wise as a dead Mex was standing in a pair of brand-new boots you just couldn't buy this side of Texas, and what would he be standing there all alone for in the first damned place?

Longarm knew he could just ask, of course. There was no law saying one couldn't stick out a hand to shake with a spinning buzz saw, either. It still wasn't always a smart move.

On the other hand, one couldn't simply draw on another man who'd given you no reason to, whether you could see his gun and gun hand under pleats of gray muslin or not. But Longarm wasn't about to turn his back on the cuss before he knew him just a mite better. So, as he ran out of places to keep walk-ing, Longarm just stopped, facing the masked and shrouded stranger with his own gun down at his side in his right fist. He nodded and tried, "Buenos dias, amigo," only to learn why they said that he who hesitates can wind up lost. For the son of a bitch fired from under his own shroud without a word of warning. So Longarm, numbly surprised to still be standing there, fired back.

He was better at hip shooting, it appeared, as the other man staggered backwards, bounced off the corner of the empty storefront, and staggered across the street, shooting down at the pavement ahead of him until he wound up against the big brass door of the consulate, rolled his back to it to face Longarm on wobbly booted ankles, and then slid down it, leaving a smeary streak that was going to call for more brass polish, even though it wasn't near as bright a shade of red as Mex mask makers used for human blood.

As Longarm moved in, covering the litter he'd deposited on Uncle Sam's doorstep, the cuss groaned inside his fake death's head and muttered, "Aw, shit, Longarm, it wasn't supposed to turn out like this, you murderous bastard!"

The heavy door opened inward, allowing the man Longarm had shot to stretch out total with his rump on the doorstep and the rest of him flat on the marble floor of the consulate vestibule. The pretty but mighty wide-eyed receptionist gal who'd come to the door for a look-see reacted to the sight at her feet much the same way a prim housewife might have to a chewed-up sparrow bird her house cat had deposited on her doorstep. As she ran off screaming blue murder Longarm took off his own costume lest the Secret Service take him for an unfriendly spook. He was tearing away at the other gent's fiesta costume when Agent Fitzroy and a couple of consulate officials joined him in the vestibule. Fitzroy holstered his own Colt Bulldog, asking, "What have we got here, Longarm?"

"Well, for openers, he's dead," replied the lawman who'd done most of the hard work, as he went on patting the well-dressed cadaver down. Hot lead had ruined his vest for all time and it smelled as if he'd pissed his pants at the last. The black three-piece suit was tailored tight, the way men who combined business in town with cows on the range wore suits and ties over riding boots. The face was unfamiliar as well as sort of waxy, now.

One of the consular paper-pushers said, "Let's haul him in all the way and shut the door, whoever he might be. This is no time to have another international incident, damn it!"

Fitzroy hunkered down to haul the head and shoulders deeper into the vestibule as Longarm unfolded the wad of paper he'd found in an inside pocket. He chuckled and said, "I doubt Mexico will care. This here's a prison release. Made out to one Mervin, a.k.a. Geek, Grogan. U.S. citizen, even if he was a convicted felon. My home office wired me to keep an eye out for him. It appears he was keeping an eye out for me, as well. But if he'd had the brains of them chickens he used to abuse he'd still be alive this minute. For I had no just cause to arrest him, even if we'd met up in the states."

Fitzroy rose back to his full height, suggesting, "You told us about him last night. I imagine someone else at that sidewalk cantina found our conversation interesting. Isn't it obvious he was waiting in ambush for you here?"

Longarm fumbled among the fold of the funeral shroud closer to the now-closed door and drew forth a nickel-plated Harrington and Richardson .32 break-open as he growled, "Now this is just plain insulting. Like I said, no brains. Or try her this way. What if he'd just been posted across the way as a lookout? He mentioned in dying that things hadn't worked out as he'd planned. I wasn't supposed to spot him and stop. I was supposed to just come in here a spell and then come back out to be trailed or maybe ambushed right by the real killer, T. J. Perkins. But this one lost his head when it looked as if I might be fixing to haul him in for questioning and— Right, no brains. Old Geek's yellow sheets run more to flimflammery than gunplay."

He found a wallet, opened it as he rose to his own feet, and added, "Plenty of I.D. All made out in his right name. He knew it was best to have his voting card and such match up with that permit to run loose they let him out of prison with. I sure wish I knew what flimflammery they had or still have in mind. Geek, here, was a specialist at pulling the wool over folk's eyes and, even with him out of the picture, I'm still wool-eyed as ever."

One of the consular cusses said he'd get the cleaning crew to do something about the mess so they could open up again, and suggested they all go back to his office for a sit-down with all cards on the table. So Longarm didn't argue. He knew that while too many cooks had been known to spoil the broth, there were times when two or more heads could think better than one.

Chapter 8

But Longarm left the consulate an hour later, by way of a sneaky side door, as confused as ever. He'd left the straw sombrero behind and meant to pick up a new costume as soon as he was able. For the rascals had somehow gotten on to the ghost duds he'd almost gotten too close to Geek Grogan in. The boys he'd just left hadn't been much help, even after he'd brought them up-to-date on everything he knew so far. The consular official who'd poured the drinks had opined the notion of contesting Paddy's Spanish grant, if she really had a Spanish grant, was just dumb. He'd asked sort of sly-voiced if Longarm had considered that the mysterious young lady, as he'd called Paddy, could be part of a plan to befuddle him. Longarm had replied that made no more sense than if she'd just bailed Perkins out to begin with and let it go at that.

As he strode along so ghostly Longarm ran that part through his masked head some more. He'd been two-timed many a time by false-hearted women, being a man and hence having little choice in such matters. But it still made no sense for them to sneak a female spy in bed with him and then take the risk of following him about as he . . . did what?

He wasn't getting anywhere. He was just one mighty confounded lawman, searching for a needle in a mighty big haystack, and now, with everyone wandering about with their faces and even general outlines masked, he could stroll right past his want and never notice. He found a hole-in-the-wall shop selling fiesta gear, from toy coffins filled with candy bones to complete costumes. He stepped inside to buy himself a whole new outfit, switching to a bloody black shroud and a silver skull. The fat old shopkeeper was mildly surprised, as Longarm changed, to see his swell customer was a gringo. He commented it was nice to see the local customs met with Anglo approval. They called you an Anglo instead of a gringo when they were trying to be nice to you.

Longarm said it had been fun, so far. Then he favored the old Mex with a lewd smile and confided, "I've heard tell that on The Day of Death some private shows are put on for the curious, everyone being masked and all."

The shopkeeper winked even lewder and said, "Sí, pero not in this part of town. Try down by the thieves' market, where the wicked señoritas put on special entertainments for a modest fee."

So Longarm picked up a pair of stout homemade zapatas while he was at it and headed back to the hotel with his new purchases.

Paddy let him in when she heard his familiar knock. But she gasped at the sight of the silver skull and would have slammed the door in his face if he hadn't been taking it off. She said, "You startled me. I was expecting another spook."

Longarm chuckled, moved over to the bed, and proceeded to remove his old stovepipe army boots. So Paddy naturally began to undress as well. But he said, "Not yet. It's early. I got to start paying more attention to the footwear of the spooks outside. I don't want anyone smart as me repaying the favor. So I'll leave these give-away boots in your safekeeping while I haunt some more in the Mex slippers I just picked up."

She naturally wanted to hear more than that. So as he changed into the rope-soled zapatas of woven leather thongs he told her, "I've been trying to picture what I'd do if I was in the zapatas of T. J. Perkins. The trouble with that is that I may have way more brains. That's gotten me in trouble before. A criminal genius is a contradiction in terms. You have to be dumb to be a crook in the first place or, if you're sly at all, you still have to have a screw loose in your head. I figure now that the want I'm after may be smart about some things but dumb about others. He's been doing what I keep telling myself not to do. He's playing chess when the name of the game is hide-and-seek."

She asked what all that had to do with Longarm stuffing his big feet in such rustic footwear. He explained, "What Perkins should have done, once you bailed him out in Nuevo Laredo, was head anywhere but where he told you and Gomez he'd be going, and then just hole up 'til I got tired out or in more trouble. He didn't. He sent for pals we were able to spot heading here as well. I haven't time to go into it right now. But that was no ruse. I know for a fact that Geek Grogan got all the way here to join him. I discounted gossip about a shady gringo getting in woman trouble in the shady parts of town because I thought it would be mighty stupid of a man on the run to mess up like that. I'd forgotten he told me to my face that he'd been turned in by a disgruntled whore in Nuevo Laredo. Some bad habits might be hard to break. Sly as he thinks he is, the cuss has this screw loose as makes him mean to whores. Few owl-hoots are. They can't afford to be. But some men, crooked or otherwise, have this romantic notion stuck in their craw that they ain't really had their way with a gal if they have to pay her. He may think he's some kind of Don Juan leaving a string of broken hearts in his wake. In point of fact he's more likely left a trail of mighty steamed shady ladies who recall him as a cheapskate who stiffed them."

Paddy grimaced and said, "He sounds charming. Remind me never to sell my fair white body to the brute."

He chuckled, stood up, and stomped about until he saw the Mex footwear fit right and made him feel a mite lighter on his feet. Paddy asked where he was headed in his ballet slippers and he said, "Whore town. It'll be running wide open today for the amusement of gents who'd never dare show up with their bare faces hanging out. The gals might be up to mischief they'd never want their mothers to know about, either. The first time I ever saw a gal going at it with a jackass in a sideshow tent, she had a mask and wig on. The jackass just had no shame."

Paddy laughed incredulously and told him that was impossible. To which he replied with a shrug, "I said it was a *freak* show. I don't care myself what's going on in whore town this afternoon. The point is that Perkins enjoys such goings on, as long as no-body asks him to pay. He got run out of such circles about the time he got here. He knows at least one pimp is as anxious to catch up with him as I am. But on a day like today, with everyone wandering around masked—"

"Goody," she cut in, "let me get dressed spooky and I'll go with you."

"You don't walk as he-spook as me. You stay here. I mean it. I got enough on my plate without having to worry about you getting in the crossfire."

"Pooh," she said, "you've opened whole new horizons to me with that eye-witness account of another gal and her big pet. But I'll be good, or bad, by myself, if you promise to get back early and show me how on earth they worked it out."

He kissed her, put his silver skull on, and ducked out into the empty hallway. He made sure the stairwell was clear before he went down as far as a side door, cracked it just wide enough to see the street outside was crowded, and slipped out to join them.

He drifted with the flow of the crowd, moving east and west, and the crowd got thinner but more purposeful as he navigated his way to the old thieves' market.

He didn't want to buy old junk some rich family had chucked out, or even something of value a house servant might have taken home to, say, polish, if it was really missed. He just had to get through the block-long clutter of pushcarts and old ladies squatting on blankets with genuine Aztec grave-jade they were willing to part with, cheap.

At the far end most of the ghouls drifting deeper into the slum looked male, whether they walked sober in their shrouds or not. They all worked deeper into the maze of narrow alleyways—it seemed a fit ending for all those lost souls. For it sure began to look as if they'd made it clean to Hell.

Naked ladies with their nipples dyed like Easter eggs leaned out of windows, barking promises of unspeakable delights to any spook that wasn't a sissy. Most of them were masked as well, as only the really pretty ones seemed content to just paint their faces funnier colors than usual. A sort of sweet-featured little thing with a blue face and a mop of purple hair asked Longarm in passing if he'd like to take part in an experiment involving two men and all of her for just twenty pesos, or, failing that, just watch for fifty centavos. When he just shook his silver skull and kept going, she called him a queer.

A little gal of about fourteen, wearing a black paper skull and nary a stitch more, followed him a ways proposing he rob her of her virginity for a modest fee. She called him even worse names when he suggested she go home and screw her dolly.

After that it got worse. He wandered into a basement cockfight, where the cleanest entertainment they had to offer consisted of chickens ripping each other apart with little steel spurs.

Longarm didn't find such stuff exciting, when all he could do was watch. So he circled the cockpit casually, checking out the footwear of the other spectators. None wore yanqui boots. So he seemed to be out the two pesos he'd paid to get in.

The next show, on the flat rooftop of a 'dobe cathouse, cost more, even though the fat gal trying to stuff herself with a writhing boa snake that seemed to want no part of her was ugly as sin, and sin could get pretty ugly in whore town when its depraved denizens really put their minds to it. Longarm never found out how the fat girl made out with that poor snake. Nobody watching wore yanqui footwear.

He paused in a smoke-filled cantina to rest his own Mex-clad feet as he gazed at other feet with more interest than usual. He ordered his beer in a bottle from the naked waitress who slithered his way. He knew the mostly German breweries down here were expected to bottle the real thing. When she came back with a bottle and clay cup, the mestizo waitress only shortchanged him two centavos and asked if he'd like to see a neat trick with the silver coin she had to give back. He suspected he knew. But he was looking for T. J. Perkins, not an argument, and stood the coin on edge on the corner of the table she indicated. He pretended to laugh when she plucked the coin from the table with her vaginal lips and strutted off triumphantly. He punched a hole through the front of his silver skull. It made breathing as well as drinking beer a lot easier.

The German lager was good, even if they did insist on calling it cerveza. Cerveza local farmers made out of corn and sour dough was just dreadful. He'd drink pulque, first, and pulque was fermented cactus juice that tasted like alcoholic spit.

He didn't think he'd better try smoking through papier-maché freshly painted with who knew what. He was running out of public places to study shoe leather. He was as likely to catch crabs as T. J. Perkins if he went into the cribs, where the putas would surely question his motives if he demanded a view of all the other customers' footgear. He'd hoped the skunk who didn't know how to get along with whores would show up at one of the shows. If he was just upstairs someplace, getting the usual services— Unless he messed up again.

Longarm called the naked waitress back, ordered

another, and this time paid with the exact change plus a modest tip he told her she could carry in her hand this time. She laughed, said she only had the one purse between her tawny thighs, and deposited it there for safekeeping, adding, "I do not always keep it stuffed with dinero, if you would like to have some fun when I get off this evening."

He said he'd try to stick around. He had to tell her something. It was sure surprising how a not bad-looking naked woman could discourage a man's natural desires by acting so unnatural.

He took his time on the second cerveza. It was early, yet. If T.J. was anywhere in the hellish but compact vice area, he might just get into another screaming match with one of the gals, and if he did . . .

Then his chain of thought was snapped by another spook sitting down across the table from him, uninvited. He could see by the way her shroud clung to her that she was built even better than the bawdy naked waitress. After that it was all guesswork. She could have had three eyes and a cleft lip under that jet-black skull she had on over her head. He just stared back with his own eye hollows, for now. He knew his American accent would give him away if he asked her what she wanted, and it seemed pretty obvious what a female spook would want with him in the middle of whore town. The infernal waitress had no doubt pointed him out as a gringo with change to spare.

The apparition's voice was soft and sort of sultry inside her grotesque headgear as she said, "You are not safe here, El Brazo Largo."

Since she obviously knew who he was, he sighed

and asked, "What gave me away? I'm not that much taller than some Mexicans I know."

"Sí. One Mexican friend you have made is called El Gato and he, too, is rather tall. He told us to look after you, should ever you come our way. Recognizing that silver skull and your new zapatas was not difficult. The shopkeeper who sold them is as devoted to La Revolucion as I am."

Longarm chuckled wryly and replied, "I'm sure glad I wasn't spotted by someone else I'm looking for. *Viva la Revolucion*, and it's about time. But I'm not down here trying to arrest old Diaz. I'd sure like to, but there are limits to my powers as a yanqui peace officer. I reckon I'm safe enough from la policia, this trip. I was invited by Mexico to pick up a gringo want. He got away from me. I got to get him back. He's said to have unwholesome interests in wicked women. So that's why I'm hunting him in this part of town. I'm not looking to mix in any other sort of trouble. So just give my regards to El Gato, next time you see him, and tell him I found his kind offer neighborly but needless, this time."

She insisted, "Idioso, even as we speak they are closing in on you. We must leave now. They will never find you where I wish for to take you."

He wanted to ask who in hell might be closing in to do what, but she was already on her feet and headed for the back door, not the front. So he drew his .44-40 and rose to trail after her, tense from head to toe. For while following a stranger could be injurious to one's health in any clime, it could get worse in this part of the world. There was just something wrong with Mexican men when it came to trusting strange women although, come to study on it, many

123

an old Texas boy had followed a gal with a rose between her teeth into a setup.

On the other hand, if she was telling the truth, he could wind up just as dead, wearing a silver skull, with no notion at all who was after him. So he waited until they were out back in a gloomy alley before he told her to plant her palms against the bricks and spread her ankles. To his mild surprise she didn't argue. If she was really part of the revolutionary movement she was no doubt used to being frisked a lot by suspicious gents she picked up in shady surroundings. There was enough daylight peeping down into the alley to keep his hands reasonably polite as he patted her down, made sure she didn't even have a weapon hidden *there* and said, "Bueno. You can't get the drop on me and I don't see any edge anyone else might have on me coming down this alley either way. So now let's talk."

"There is not time," she insisted. "We have to get you to the far side of the railroad yards in broad daylight!"

That sounded like a piss-poor place to set up an ambush. So he said, "All right. You go first and keep it in mind that you're not armed and I am. If I go down, you go down with me. I mean it."

She said soberly, "We know you are not a man for to trifle with. Follow me and— Wait, I think we ought to see if we can make it harder for them by exchanging these skulls."

That made sense. So he didn't argue and he was pleasantly surprised when she took her black skull off to swap it for his silver one. For like his old pal, El Gato, whatever El Gato might be to her, she was way more Spanish than Indian. Maybe pure Spanish in her case. For her wavy hair was auburn and her wide-set eyes were the color of Aztec jade. She smiled up at him in a manner to suggest she was pleasantly surprised as well. Some of the yarns her folk spun about El Brazo Largo had no doubt led her to expect a meaner-looking cuss.

As they went on their way, her now silver-skulled and him black all over, he asked how come they'd done that if it had been pals of hers who'd said he was wandering about so silver today. She explained, "I am not as worried about them spotting you as I am them spotting me. We take every precaution, but the government pays so much for information and our people are so poor—"

"El Gato told me you had to watch out for tattle-tales," he cut in. "How come we have to cross the railyards?"

She asked, incredulously, "Do you take me for one of the women who live near the thieves' market? My people are poor, but not indecent. We are trying to reach a working-class neighborhood la policia take little interest in."

He agreed that might offer a swell place for rebels to plot, adding, "I understand Sam Adams, Paul Revere, and such plotted the Boston Tea Party above a respectable waterfront hangout called the Green Dragon. The redcoats paid little attention to the dock workers drinking downstairs. Lawmen are more inclined to poke their noses into sinister places that really look sinister."

But when they got there, after stumbling over a wide expanse of sunbaked tracks that made him itch like hell between the shoulder blades, Longarm was surprised to find himself following her up a ladder into what looked to be a railroad switch tower.

When he joined her up in the middle of the air he saw the glassed-in enclosure had been fitted with a brass bedstead, a cooking range and other comforts. He removed his black skull with a puzzled smile and said, "I give up. I thought the national railroads of Mexico were the personal property of El Presidente and that you folk were out to overthrow him, railroads and all."

She removed her own skull, saying, "We are, no matter how the fake election he's staging this year turns out. Diaz stole this particular branch of his railroad empire as he stole all the others, without thinking, as a shark devours its prey. Until then the various railroads were in competition with, how you say, duplicate facilities? This tower is no longer needed for to run trains in and out of the yards. A lot of things those ladrones seized from their rightful owners are no longer used for anything. Diaz just keeps everything, like an old woman with more jewels than she can ever wear, see?"

Longarm cast a glance all about through the glassed-in vantage point, saying, "I swan. This is so simple it just has to work. Here we are, forted up like eagles in plain sight of any yard workers with no instructions about this old tower they're so used to walking right on past, right?"

She dimpled demurely and said, "If they know what is good for them. Diaz does not allow trade unions, but we have a railroad workers' union anyway. Nobody will bother us here, and as you see, nobody can get near us without crossing open yards in all directions."

126

"Swell. How do we get out of this cabin in the sky if they do just that?"

She assured him they wouldn't, adding, "There are certain rules to this game we play with Diaz and his ladrones. They stay clear of certain parts of town they have no business in and we make fewer riots. It's not la policia, whom you said you had some understanding with, El Brazo Largo. It's a bandito leader, we think, who has put a price on your head. The word has been spread that you are worth mucho dinero, dead, to wicked men who deal in stolen jewels. As you know, alas, there are men willing to kill a strange Anglo for his boots alone, and we do not control all the guns in this country that the government does not control."

He nodded soberly and said, "I noticed. I just shot it out with a cuss called Geek in front of the U.S. Consulate. But I can't hardly catch the wanted killer I'm after by sitting up here in a glass box, grand as the view may be."

"We know. You are searching for a gringo called Teem by others who search for him as well. He seems to be muy malo. Even our wicked people wish to see him dead. We have let it be known that this Teem Perkins will hang just as high if he is delivered into the hands of El Brazo Largo. I am not sure he will be delivered alive. But with you, la policia, and people la policia usually look for looking for Teem, how long do you think he can remain at liberty?"

"Call me Custis. It's shorter. I'd hate to be in old T.J.'s zapatas right now if half what you say is true. Meanwhile, how long do you reckon we're stuck here and how might you be called?"

"True names are not important in La Revolucion.

127

I am called Mariposa by my friends." He resisted the impulse to call her Butterfly, in English, since that sounded even dumber.

She asked if he would give her until nightfall to lead him to the hideout or remains of T. J. Perkins. He said that was the best offer he'd had all day and she said, "Bueno," and sat on the bed to slip off her funeral shroud.

He gulped as she did so. For he'd been picturing her up to now as having at least a slip on under that raggedy muslin. But she was stark naked, save her pumps and black stockings, and auburn-haired all over, as she cast the ghostly garb aside to say simply, "Are you still worried about how we might pass the short time we may have together, ever?"

He said, "Viva la Revolucion!" but still made certain the trap door they'd come up through was bolted down securely before he even took off his gun rig. The rest soon followed, of course, but as he joined her naked on the bed with the sunlight streaming on her cameo curves and soft auburn hair, he felt obliged to ask her, gently, if she knew just what she was about to start, warning, "I'm a tumbleweed man, even up in the states, and, no offense, you're a sweet little gal for just loving and leaving."

She took him in her arms, in a gentle way, as she crooned, "We are all tumbleweeds caught in the winds of change. I was a virgin when I joined La Revolucion. Since then I have learned for to enjoy each moment of life the movement allows me."

So he rolled aboard her beautiful as well as welcome-home body and for now forgot all else as their own movement occupied their full attention. She climaxed ahead of him, more than once, in a manner to indicate she hadn't been getting as much of late. When they had to rest their lungs, at least, by relaxing entwined as one, she smiled up at him like a sweet little kid who'd been given a swell present and panted, "I am so happy. Everything they say about you seems to be true, after all. I feared some of the other *adelitas* were just bragging."

He almost asked a dumb question. Then he kissed her as he recalled adelita was rebel slang for the gals who trudged along after the riders, on both sides, when Mex politics were being discussed on the battlefield. He hated to picture a sweet little gal like this one packing food and ammo all day and getting passed around as one soldado she was assigned to got shot in his own inevitable turn. But that was the way things were and they'd doubtless stay that way until old Diaz got licked or, hell, just died of old age. The latter seemed most likely. Diaz had been a hell of a guerrilla fighter under Juarez. He was only fifty-odd, and at the rate things were going, Mariposa and her pals would be fifty-odd by the time they got rid of Diaz, if he didn't get rid of them first. He knew better than to try and talk a devoted rebel gal out of going on so stubborn. So he started moving in her some more. In a hundred years it wouldn't seem as important who'd gotten to run Mexico. But in the meantime, every stolen hour of loving had its own no-nonsense value a man, or woman, could store for keeps in the treasure chest of memory. As if she was a mind reader, Mariposa murmured, "By this time, mañana, you will have forgotten all about me. Pero I do not think I will ever forget this short sweet time in the arms of El Brazo Largo."

He reminded her his name was Custis and assured

her he felt sure that someday when he was an old retired lawman rocking on some damned old porch he'd no doubt have plenty of time to look back on all the gals he'd got to kiss and that sooner or later she'd have to come up as one of the best kissers. He didn't think she wanted to hear, as he'd already noticed, that men dreaming back dreamed most about the gals they'd never gotten anywhere with. Adelita as the nickname of a camp follower came from a sad old Spanish song about a gal named Adelita who'd got shot before her poor soldado got to screw her as much as he'd wanted.

But there was nothing in his way as far as this sweet adelita went, so the next hour or so passed pleasant as well as all too quickly. Longarm didn't remember falling asleep in Mariposa's soft arms, but he knew he had when he suddenly found himself off the bed with his .44-40 trained on the trap door.

Then he heard the funny clicking again, behind him, and spun about to cover the sidewinder or whatever that had crawled into bed with them. Only it wasn't that, either. Mariposa was sitting up cross-legged with a bitty telegraph set. It looked more like a rat trap in her naked lap. She sort of looked as if she was playing naughty with herself as she worked the key with the heel of her palm resting against her auburn pubic hairs. A coiled wire ran over one tawny thigh to the battery boxes he figured had to be under the bed. La Revolucion sure was getting fancy-pants of late. It made him feel better about hiding out so public.

Longarm could follow International Morse and his Spanish was tolerable. But he couldn't follow both at the same time, albeit he picked up Perkins when

Mariposa tapped it out, listened, and they both read the answer as "Sí."

Mariposa and her unseen rebel pal tapped back and forth some more. Then she signed off to sit there staring up at him mighty wistful. She said, "I told you we had spread the word. Perkins is being hunted by common criminals as well. Word gets around muy pronto. A leading light of our underworld wants *out*. He wishes to know if you would be willing to make a deal with him. He wishes to turn the gringo ladrone he never liked to begin with over to you, in exchange for your word you will forget all about him and his jewelry business."

Longarm sat down beside her and put his gun back in its bedposted holster, saying, "Hell yes, I have no jurisdiction over purely Mex crooks."

She sighed and said, "I know. That is what I just told my friends to tell his friends. You will be taken to him during la siesta, when even la policia are indoors with their shirts off and their feet up." She glanced out the tower glass at the high hot sun, sighed again, and said, "La siesta may start a little late, because of the fiesta. But no later than half past noon or a quarter to one. I told them to come for you at one. Do you think we could manage for to come, at least one more time?"

He said he sure aimed to try and she went along with dog style as the quickest way to get there, even if she did say it made her feel less romantico. As he stood his bare feet on the plank floor to grip a hipbone in either hand and proceed to pleasure her more practical than romantic, he had a grand view of the empty sunbaked railyards all around and assured her he was sure nobody would catch her in such an awkward position. Then he mused, half to himself, "I can't say I cotton to the notion of wandering to a meeting with who knows who in broad-ass daylight. A rooftop rifle carries close to a mile when you can see who you're aiming at."

She arched her spine and gritted her teeth as she replied, "Oh, faster, querido! Nobody will try for you in the company of a rebel guide. Not if they wish to remain open for business near the thieves' market. The hombre who wishes for to rid himself of a too-hot business associate is a long-established, how you say, fence? He did not say what his business with Perkins had been, up to now. He just said that now he would like to end it and go back to vending stolen jewelry in peace."

"Does he have la policia fixed?" asked Longarm with a deep thrust.

"Of course. That is no doubt why he wants to rid himself of any connections with an hombre la policia are not protecting. You seem to have the approval of the government as far as taking Perkins back goes. Oh, go faster! It must be this charade Diaz is holding for to convince outsiders we have fair elections down here and— Madre de mia! Turn me over and finish off *right*!"

So he did, and whatever fate she was meant to meet up with in the end, they both knew this was the finish as far as the two of them could ever mean to one another. So they both did their best to make it a good one, and it was.

Chapter 9

The youth they sent to lead Longarm into further temptation was bare of head and foot and dressed more raggedy-ass than like a spook. Mariposa agreed with him that Longarm might do better with his fiesta costume just folded over one arm for now, since most of the certified walking dead were resting up off the sunbaked streets for a real hoedown with fireworks and likely some real corpses in the cool of a post-siesta evening.

That left Longarm bareheaded as well. But working-class Mexicans were more likely than his kind to go about hatless, so he put the Stetson he'd left at the hotel out of his mind, once he'd followed his guide across the wide-open yards and into the maze beyond without getting picked off by some rascal with a .52-200 and a scope sight.

The kid leading him wherever allowed he answered to Chino and didn't seem to want to talk any more than that about himself. So Longarm had him figured as a go-between working with the crooks ahead, or a rebel who'd guessed how a durned old gringo had just spent the last few hours with Mariposa.

It didn't matter, in the end. Chino pointed at a bitty blue door set in a mighty thick 'dobe wall and lit out without saying so much as a good-bye. Longarm shrugged, looked both ways, and, seeing he had the mysterious little door all to himself, drew his six-gun and tried the latch.

The door wasn't locked. Longarm stepped into the near total darkness on the far side and slid his back along the stucco to make sure he had no pinpoints of light outlining him before he called out, "Well, here I am and name your pleasure."

There was no reply. Longarm stared into the gloom as his eyes adjusted, muttering, "They might have told me a damned old bat that only comes out at night wanted a meeting."

As the mysterious black blobs all about him began to turn into boxes and barrels, piled high and bound together by cobwebs, Longarm decided he had to be in the back of someone's warehouse. He started easing forward to see who or what might be lurking up front.

But as he came to a cross aisle an overhead Edison bulb flicked on to illuminate him, the nearest packing crates all around, and not much else. Longarm naturally crawfished back into a darker slot, calling out conversationally, "It's nice to see how up-to-date you are. Would you like to come out come out wherever you are, or do you want me to shoot out that newfangled lamp and start from scratch?"

A familiar figure stepped from between the crates on the far side of the circle of light. It was Lawyer Gomez from Nuevo Laredo. The dapperly dressed Mex rolled a nail keg out under the light on its rim and sat on it before he said, "My present client does not wish for to meet you in person, Deputy Long. I have, as you see, been retained for to speak for him. Would you like to put that cannon away now?"

"Not hardly. I feel more comfortable with it trained on you. I hope you savvy what happens to you should one or more of these boxes all about burst into flames or something."

Gomez looked hurt and said, "I reproach you for having such unkind suspicions of a simple country lawyer. You were told this was to be a peaceful meeting between, how you say, men of the world?"

Longarm moved closer, but said, "I was told the gent who wanted to deal was a famous crook, too. You sure get around, Gomez."

The Mex lawyer shrugged and replied, "I go where my services are required. My present client does not wish to become any more famous than he is. He sees no need for you to know who he is and I, as his legal adviser, agree that might be best. Since neither of us is in the position to turn the other over to the law on either side of the border, shall we proceed?"

Longarm leaned against a crate, as far into the light as he meant to show himself, and allowed he was all ears.

Gomez said, "I shall deny this if you ever try to use it against me. But as you must have already guessed, I got Perkins out of that rurale post because he was naturally no use there to his Mexican business associates."

Longarm nodded grimly and asked, "Where does the girl and that bull about old Spanish land grants come in?"

Gomez looked pained and answered simply, "The corrupt officer in command demanded more so-called bail money than expected. The girl from Nuevo Mejico had been sent to me by her own law firm on the other matter. It was pure good fortune. She and her gringo lawyers had expected for her to cross at El Paso–Juarez. I enjoy a modest reputation along the border as a quick fixer, so—"

"So you fixed her swell by letting her bail us both out, at higher than usual cost, with her own money," Longarm cut in. It was a statement rather than a question.

Gomez shrugged and replied innocently, "It is well known you people have more discretionary income than my people. As you may have guessed, I had to string la señorita along just a little for to get Perkins out. I tell you frankly that I did not and do not care about her or her ancient legal problems. I simply told her she might get you to escort her here to Ciudad Mejico if—"

"I savvy that bullshit," Longarm cut in with a weary wave of his gun muzzle. "Get to here and now. Your client never bailed out a gringo ladrone because he admired Perkins's big blue eyes."

Gomez chuckled and replied, "My client prefers women as objects of admiration. He thought, although I warned him otherwise, that Perkins might be of some use to him in the disposal of certain, ah, objects of art."

"Don't you mean stolen jewelry?" Longarm asked.

The dapper lawyer replied with another reproachful look, "That is none of your concern, yanqui. Anything stolen outside your U.S. jurisdiction is, well, out of your jurisdiction."

Longarm snorted in disgust and said, "Bueno, your mysterious client has things fixed with the local law. Get to the part about fixing Perkins, and tell me why he needs so much fixing all of a sudden. Your pals could have fixed him good just by letting me pick him up at the border. We've got hangmen standing in line to fix that old boy. How come you don't love him no more?"

Gomez said simply, "He is a loose cannon on the deck. I told them they were making a big mistake in recruiting him for serious business. He is better known along the border as an hombre of sudden passions and little common sense."

Longarm nodded and said, "You'll get no argument from me about that. The two pals he had tagging along didn't strike me as all that professional. Swan diving when there's no water in the pool or acting trigger-happy across from the U.S. Consulate just ain't my notion of how Frank and Jesse might have gone about it."

"It gets worse. The idiot can't get along with our people, either. He has managed to involve himself in a very dangerous as well as stupid blood feud with a vice ring we have no understanding with. Worse yet, when my client tried to chide him about his lack of gallantry with women, Perkins, how you say, threw down on him?"

Longarm whistled softly and said, "I follow your drift. I doubt I'd want to set up a big jewel operation with a gent who kept getting in hot water and waving guns in my face. So how do you boys mean to deliver him to me?"

Gomez looked away and murmured, "That is where we are open to suggestions. We managed to separate him from the gringo gun hands he still has left by sending them on other business. He was to meet us here this afternoon. As you see, he has not shown up. He may simply be late, in which case my client begs you not to shoot this place up more than you really need to. If he does not show up, it will mean, of course, that he suspects some sort of treachery."

Longarm chuckled dryly and replied, "Treachery from *you* swell gents? Now why should anyone suspect that? You say your boss crook had a flare-up with Perkins, involving the waving about of weaponry. He knows I'm in town and what happened to two of his gun-toting pals. Putting myself in such uncomfortable shoes, I'd say he's already caught a train to parts unknown."

"He can't," said Gomez simply. "We have our own friends watching all the ticket windows. He may be spending la siesta with some puta who has not heard he hates to pay and punches women who ask. *Quien sabe?* He may even show up here, any time now. If he was not a drooling idiot you and me would not be holding this pleasant conversation, eh?"

Longarm followed that drift, too, albeit he didn't like where they seemed to be drifting. The warehouse was stuffy as well as dark and stinky. He wouldn't have wanted to spend the time in a cool taproom, drinking with the likes of Gomez. He said, "I got a better plan. A quicker one, leastways. If you sent word for Perkins to meet us here, you must have had a place to send it." Then he lay his six-gun handy on the edge of a waist-high crate and got out his notebook and stub pencil, adding, "I'm listening."

Gomez said, "He is with a woman we do not wish to see involved with the law."

"Gals as set an owlhoot up don't get hung as a

rule. Don't play games with me, Gomez. It was your notion to meet with me about your loose cannon. I ain't here because I just love to lurk in strange gloomy places with my back feeling itchy. If you can't produce the cuss or even tell me where he is, I'd best be on my way."

He started to put the notebook away when Gomez said, "Wait. You must understand the woman is of good family, a widow dwelling in a respectable neighborhood. The capture, your word, will be most discreet?"

Longarm shrugged and replied, "I'm a peace officer, not a string of firecrackers. I make arrests peaceable as I'm allowed to. If he comes quiet, I'll take him quiet. If he wants a noisy shoot-out, well, the lady's reputation will be on his head, not mine. Give me the damned address. Gunplay attracts the most attention after dark and it's getting late for bullshitting."

The address Gomez gave him was on the far side of downtown. So Longarm dropped by the hotel to get rid of his spook outfit and put on his proper hat. He filled Paddy in and told her to get dressed, packed, and ready to move sudden, explaining, "If I ain't been sent on a snipe hunt I ought to have Perkins, one way or another, in time for us to catch the evening northbound to Juarez. Santa Fe is a mite out of our way, but I got to see you safely home and maybe get to the bottom of this bull about that cattle king and your old land grant."

She clapped her hands and said, "Goody! But isn't Santa Fe a mite more than a mite out of your way, darling? I thought they wanted to hang that nasty T.J. in New Orleans."

Longarm nodded and explained, "They do. They'd like to hang him at Fort Smith and Fort Collins as well. But if I haul him back to Denver he gets to stand trial before they can hang him. And I figure it's only right to try a man before you hang him, and I was sent by Denver to begin with. So find your old gray bonnet with the blue ribbons on it and we'll go for a ride with a slayer."

She winced, told him puns were the lowest form of humor, and asked if Gomez had said anything new about her land grant.

He shook his head impatiently and said, "They were just using you, Paddy. We'll worry about why Caleb Woodward started the fool dispute to begin with when I get you and Perkins back to New Mexico. I can't do that standing here. So adios, you pretty thing."

He checked the address again as he was going down the stairs. He wasn't at all happy about the *camino* the house number went with. He'd forgotten the number that old Rosalinda had jotted down for him that time. But how many Camino Oros could there be in one town, even a big one?

As he made his way through streets broad and narrow, still deserted because of la siesta, he saw he was indeed passing the same landmarks. It was after three, now, and some of the ghosts were commencing to haunt the streets again, albeit more than one adult had now given up the ghost in favor of regular streetwear. One had to be a kid on The Day of Death to stay dead all day, it would seem. Nobody seemed to pay much attention to Longarm's dark suit and

Stetson. In such a fashionable neighborhood lots of high-toned Mex gents dressed sort of gringo, and Longarm's Anglo-Saxon but well-tanned features didn't stand out so much among gents of pure Spanish extraction.

As he trudged on, checking house numbers from time to time, Longarm spied an all-too-familiar church tower ahead and groaned to himself, "Aw, no, Lord. I just don't want to hear about it if I've been going sloppy seconds to a dog like T. J. Perkins. I just finished putting the Robles family down as a pack of harmless shoestring legal hacks."

But as he checked the house numbers again he saw the Robles place had to be way this side of the address Gomez had given him. He was just starting to feel good about that when Rosalinda in the flesh, with her pretty face painted white and her curves partly hidden under whispy black flutters, yoo-hooed to him from the far side of the street and catty-cornered over to join him, saying, "La siesta just ended, if you were on your way to where I hope you were on your way, you silly. I am on my way to a party. I have to show up, whether I have to stay late or not. Would you like to come along as my escort? We could say you disguised yourself as a gringo, no?"

Longarm chuckled fondly down at her and said, "I'd sure like to, querida. It sounds safer, even if it's a lousy party. But as a matter of fact I'm on my way to another señorita's place."

He saw he'd hurt her by putting it so clumsy and quickly told her, "To meet a wanted man, not any other woman I might want."

Rosalinda looked less pale under her chalk-white makeup and even managed a timid smile as she replied, "In that case I must forgive you. I was afraid you were annoyed at me for getting so silly the other night. I usually don't drink that much. Did I do anything ridiculous? When I came to my senses you had already left. I was afraid I might have said or done something for to annoy you."

He assured her, "You hardly annoyed me, Rosalinda. As a matter of fact, I had a grand time. At least, I think I did. Like you said, we both got pretty sloshed."

She smiled up at him demurely to say, "I think I must have been drunk indeed. The next morning, as I bathed, I noticed some bruises. I am glad to hear you remember nothing really silly taking place. I must go now, Custis. Perhaps we shall meet again before you have to leave for el norte?"

He said perhaps and so they shook on it and parted friendly. He knew some night when he was stuck alone in a bedroll on the open range he was sure to recall Rosalinda fondly. For it was seldom a gent met a gal who screwed so fine and let it drop so sensible. He knew that she knew that he knew she was there for the asking if he wanted more, while, at the same time, she wouldn't be holding her breath and likely figured on getting sort of drunk and silly, as fate permitted, before she got too old and fat for such good things to happen. It was a crying shame that most gals couldn't enjoy life like most men did.

He passed the old church. The house numbers to either side were still way too low, and how much farther could El Camino Oro run, for Pete's sake? Had he known he'd have to walk this far he'd have hired a damned caballo.

Then, as the numbers were getting more reasonable, he passed a walled-in burial plot next to yet another and even older 'dobe church, so crumbled it had to be left over from the early mission days. The low-slung flat-roofed house across the way had the same number over its carved oaken door as Longarm had written in his notebook. He kept walking without changing stride. For there was nothing like a stranger pausing out front to stare at a house when it came to catching the attention, and bullets, of anyone lurking inside on the prod.

He strode on up to the next corner and swung around it to consider his options. Perkins had been sent word to meet his pals at that warehouse. If he was too suspicious to answer a message from pals, there was just no saying how he'd respond to the law pounding on his front door. There had to be a better way.

There was. There were no telegraph poles down the alley behind this particular row of houses, but there was a back gate, meant as a service entrance from the alley. Better yet, it was old and dried out, with cracks worth peering through. Longarm put one eye to the gap between the jamb and rusty hinges. He saw the place had a walled-in back garth instead of a patio. The house was smaller than Rosalinda's, and just took up an L of the lot. There was nobody out back. From the way the garden had gone to weeds it hardly seemed likely they spent much time back this way. Longarm got out his pocketknife. The simple wrought-iron latch was a cinch. He put his knife away, hauled out his .44-40, and moved in.

He crossed the yard in a silent gunfighter's crouch, the muzzle of his six-gun trying to make up its mind between the back door and the four shuttered windows staring back. Nothing happened. He flattened out between the door and a shuttered back window—a mite tense, of course—and now that nobody inside could see him without coming out, the odds against him were a heap less hairy.

Lots of folk he'd busted in on in the past had been dumb enough to worry about the front entrance while forgetting to watch the back. But Perkins had established he was fast and sneaky. Longarm considered himself more upright and honest, and he still knew a dozen ways to turn a back door into a sucker-trap.

He didn't want to get doused with a bucket of water or catch a bellyful of buckshot from a shotgun gin. That door likely led out from the kitchen. Other chambers would be farther out along the two legs of the L. He knew Spanish architects paid more attention to Mother Nature than the fancy-dans who put up Victorian houses meant to pass for scaled-down castles or oversized steamboats. Not having as much to spend on fighting nature indoors, Mex builders tried to work with the way winds blew and the sun rose and set. They liked to put bedrooms facing the sunrise so the first light of dawn could wake folk up, and the same room would then be facing away from the hot afternoon sun and be the coolest in the house at bedtime. Longarm did his best to figure out the interior layout, Mex style. Then he made for the east-facing window farthest from the likely kitchen in a low crouch. If Perkins knew la siesta was over he'd be in yet another part of the house. If he didn't care, he'd likely be laid out slugabed. Either way beat busting into a kitchen via a more usual entrance.

Like most shuttered windows, this one's slatted shutters swung out and likely latched from the inside with one of those wrought-iron s-shaped latches you just gave half a twist to. Longarm listened sharp. He heard funny noises coming out through the slats. The wood was old and half rotted. He gingerly twisted a bottom slat that looked more rotted than the others. Six or more inches twisted off in his strong fingers. The soft sounds inside didn't change. He hunkered down for a peek-through. He saw that, sure enough, a gal lay facedown across a bed, sobbing fit to bust. He didn't have to worry about her packing concealed weapons. She lay there naked as a jay. Her ass wasn't bad, either.

Longarm opened the latch from outside with his knife blade. The gal on the bed never noticed until he was rolling his own rump over the sill, with his six-gun trained politely but firmly in her general direction. She raised her teary red face from the rumpled sheets to gasp in surprise and terror. He was surprised, too. The gal was brunette, but after that she looked more Irish than Mex. He told her softly, "Don't yell. I ain't after you, ma'am. I am U.S. Deputy Custis Long, in case you didn't know. I gave my word to leave you out of it if I could. So don't make me include you in, savvy?"

She groped some of the sheet over her, sobbing, "Then Tim was right. They did mean to throw him to the wolves, the two-faced greasers!"

Longarm got himself all the way in, closed the shutter behind him, and lowered his gun muzzle more politely as he nodded at her in the more modest light to say, "They sure did. Where is he? Anyone can see he ain't here."

She sat up as if she figured her nipples might not be all that noticeable in the semi-darkness, and told

Longarm, "You just missed him. We just made love for the last time and I already miss him, damn you!"

Longarm shrugged and said, "I'd heard he was quite a hand with the ladies. Most of 'em seem to have wound up madder at him, but maybe he don't mistreat such pretty Americano gals. I want you to listen sharp before you answer, Miss . . . never mind. Do I have your full attention?"

She nodded, as if resigned to anything, and said, "I guess I can oblige you, if it means you'll let me go. I may as well confess he left me sort of hot and—"

"I ain't looking to get laid. I'm looking for T. J. Perkins. If you'd like to tell me which way he went, you'll find I never arrest a friendly witness. If you aim to give him a lead on me by leading me down the primrose path, it's only fair to warn you I mean to carry *some* damned American owlhoot back to the states with me. And if you ain't an owlhoot you'll just have your chance to prove that in a federal court, so what's it going to be?"

She lowered her lashes and said, "He went to church, across the way. I know it sounds crazy. But that's where he went. He said he wanted to confess his sins and never to expect him back. If you want my honest opinion, this seems a mighty dumb time for him to be taking up religion. But that's what he said."

Longarm started to tell her she was loco en la cabeza. But since she'd already agreed it sounded sort of crazy, he nodded and said, "I know where the church is and, damn it, I've been doing my level best to take the cuss without exiting the rest of Mexico. He was packing his gun, of course?"

146

The naked gal on the bed nodded bleakly. Long-arm swore under his breath and left the way he'd entered, by way of the window, back yard and alley. For he wasn't about to step out the front door facing the entrance to the old church in such swell light for shooting.

Churches had more than one entrance as well. It only took Longarm a few minutes to work around to a side door that wasn't even locked. Inside, he paused to get his bearings in the perfumed gloom. As he stood behind a massive pillar he saw that a heap of neighborhood folk had drifted in after la siesta. That seemed only natural on a feast day. None of the worshippers had come to church looking dead. Long-arm knew it was his duty to keep things that way. Some of the heads bowed in the semi-darkness of the old church belonged to little kids. On the far side he could make out the boxed-in confessionals. It hardly seemed likely the old gent saying mass near the ba-roque gilt-wood altar could be hearing confessions at the same time. There was no way to just stride over, gun leveled, without messing up the services consid-erable. Longarm had too much respect for all reli-gions to do that. So he started easing along the side aisle to cross over near the front entrance and ease down the other aisle. He figured if he took a pew seat and kept his bare head bowed he could likely cover those oaken boxes until someone less holy came out. As he worked his way around he sized the whole crowd up. The cuss had told his play-pretty he meant to drop in here on his way to wherever. That didn't mean he hadn't been surprised by the late-afternoon mass. He could be anywhere among those innocent neighborhood folk. Longarm noticed the cameo features of a young mother with her head bowed next to a little kid and muttered, "Damn you, T.J. This just ain't a proper place for a wanted killer to hole up!"

He got to the almost deserted area near the holy water font by the open front entrance. It would have been deserted more if a sweet-faced young nun hadn't been standing there with her hands folded inside her sleeves, Chinese style. He nodded at her as pleasantly as he could manage and put his gun away, for now. She said softly, "Pero no, El Brazo Largo! This is a house of God."

Longarm nodded again and said, "I'm aware of that, Sister. Before we get into an argument about sanctuary, is it safe to assume that since you know who I am, you know who I'm looking for on these premises?"

She sighed and said, "Si. There are certain limits to the right to sanctuary. Despite what the poor confused Calvin said about us, we are not a criminal organization. Señor Perkins has had this explained to him. All we have promised him is that we shall not allow him to be butchered like a beast on hallowed ground. Do I have your promise on that, El Brazo Largo?"

Longarm hesitated. Then he said, "Sister, I consider my word my bond, even when I ain't offering it to a woman of the cloth. So I'm only prepared to say I won't shoot first. I can't offer better than that. I just can't act otherwise."

She dimpled and said, "That sounds more Lutheran than Calvinistic. Pero, no matter. Follow me."

He did. He expected her to lead him somewhere else inside the church. But she opened a side door to step out into the sunlit graveyard instead. She pointed at a sort of stone doghouse in a far corner and said, "He is hiding in that tomb, poor thing. He says he does not wish for to make a fight of it. He says too many people are after him and that his own friends have betrayed him. We told him you had spoken to Padre Filipe over at Fourteen Holy Martyrs about a peaceful ending to this madness. He knows, as we know, that El Brazo Largo is not as some of them who also hunt him may well be. Allow me to go first. I think he trusts me."

But Longarm said, "Hold on, Sister. I don't want you between us in the crossfire should he have second thoughts!"

But the young nun just nodded and said, "I know. Neither of you are as likely to fire with my body between you."

And then she was off and almost running between the old iron crosses and weathered stone angels. So Longarm legged after her, protesting, "Damn it, Sister, oops, sorry, you've no call to take a chance like this for the U.S. Justice Department."

But she kept going, saying, "I am not doing this for anyone but my husband, Jesus. My mortal flesh is less important than the sanctity of this holy place. Surely you can see that?"

Longarm could only reply he sure hoped the cuss holed up in that old tomb could. As they got closer he stepped to one side to take cover behind a stone lady with wings and cover the gaping doorway without having to shoot through a lady made of brave as well as mortal flesh as he called out, "All right, old son. Toss your gun out. If you make me upset this nice little gal I swear I'll still haul you out of there alive with at least two busted kneecaps, hear?"

A six-gun fluttered end-over-end in the sunlight to alight in the dust near the black hem of the young nun's habit. Then the wily-eyed cuss appeared in the doorway, with both hands held high. He grinned wearily at the two of them and said, "Well, you can't say I didn't give you a good run for your money, Longarm. But a man gets tired of running and—"

"Never mind all that," Longarm cut in. Turning to the nun he asked, "Sister, could you leave us in private now? I got to search this hombre before I take step-one in his treacherous company."

She nodded but pleaded softly, "You will not, how you say, whip him with your pistol?"

Longarm smiled at her sincerely and said, "I won't even turn him over my knee and spank him, as long as he behaves." So she nodded and turned to go. But Longarm called out, "Muchas gracias, Mujer del Cristo!"

"Por nada, señores," she replied.

So Longarm nudged his prisoner and said, "Thank the lady, damn you."

The less couth owlhoot shrugged and asked, "For what? You was out to take me alive to begin with, wasn't you?"

Longarm shoved him inside the tomb, growling, "Don't bet on it. Face the wall, weight on your palms and feet spread. You know the drill by now."

The ugly mutt did. But as Longarm patted him down he laughed and said, "Don't get fresh. I ain't that sort of a boy. What did you expect me to be packing, the crown jewels of England? If I wasn't just about broke I'd still be running, you sap."

Longarm had to agree there wasn't more than a few days' eating money in the desperado's wallet. He put it in his own pocket, seeing old T.J. would be living on the bounty of the Justice Department from here on. They gave Longarm twelve cents a mile to transport prisoners and there was many a mile still ahead of them. He got rid of a jackknife, let his prisoner keep a pocket kerchief in case he felt like weeping, and asked him how come he used expensive rubbers when Mex brands sold so much cheaper. The rascal leaning against the wall chuckled and said, "If you knew the old whore I was just shacked up with you wouldn't ask. There are times a man just can't risk a rubber with a hole in it."

Longarm grimaced and said, "She seemed fonder of you. You just don't like anybody, do you? Put your hands down behind you. I want you cuffed before I introduce you to the lady we'll be traveling north with. If you talk dirty to her she'll have my permit, and the ability, to slap your ugly mutt."

Chapter 10

Longarm waited until their northbound train pulled out of the yards after dark. Then he sent Paddy to powder her nose or whatever, and as soon as he and the prisoner were alone he said, "All right, strip."

T.J. didn't argue. He'd been arrested serious before. But as he stood in the narrow space between the swaying seat he kept bitching, even as he shed his duds, that they were on the wrong train. Longarm told him to just keep shucking and let other folk worry about the timetables and maps. T.J. got down to his socks, turned about a time or two for inspection with his stinky armpits exposed, and asked if Longarm was satisfied now. His captor replied, "No. Bend over and spread your cheeks. Take off them socks, too."

Once he'd satisfied himself that the slicker wasn't even concealing cooties big enough to be dangerous, Longarm handed T.J. a paper bag as he kicked everything his prisoner had removed into a pile just below the window, saying, "I picked up some travel duds for you. Put 'em on. Then set so I can cuff and leg-iron you."

As T.J. tore open the bag he protested, "This shit ain't nothing for a white man to wear. How come you want me dressed like an infernal Mex farmboy in white pajamas and rope-soled sandals for Pete's sake?"

"Pete has nothing to do with it," Longarm replied. "I'm lazy as well as careful." Then, covering the prisoner as he got him into the simple peon outfit, Longarm opened the window with his free hand to chuck everything T.J. had been wearing, from the boots up, out to the four winds, saying, "Someone drifting along the tracks in the morning will surely admire such fine gringo garb, and it don't matter to us what else they find hidden in a seam or a hollow boot heel. I'll be surprised as hell if you find so much as a watch spring suitable for picking locks in them humble but brand-new duds I picked up at the market with this very trip in mind."

As Longarm chained his prisoner's bare ankles and cuffed one wrist to an armrest, T.J. muttered, "They must have told you I was some kind of escaping wonder."

"They sure did. I'd ask how you got the drop on those customs agents in New Orleans if I thought the truth was in you. Suffice it to say you won't find me half as careless. I'm sorry about the leg irons. I ain't as chickenshit when I'm transporting one of you boys lonesome. Can't take chances with you taking it in your head to kick a lady in the shins to get me all confused."

Longarm returned to his seat across from T.J. as he reholstered his six-gun, adding, "She ought to be back any minute now. I can't say I'm looking forward to the three of us just staring at each other from here to Juarez, but it was your own notion to take up a life of crime."

The prisoner licked his lips nervously and said, "I

never agreed to go to *Juarez* with anybody, damn it. The deal was for you to return me for trial in New Orleans, remember?"

Longarm shook his head and replied, "That may be the way you remember it. I don't recall offering anyone a thing but a trip back to the states. New Orleans would be way out of my way, even if I hadn't promised to see a lady home as we pass through New Mexico Territory."

T.J. blustered, "Damn it, I'm wanted for murder and worse in New Orleans!"

"There ain't nothing worse than murder, and you done that, first and federal, in Colorado. The Denver District Court is closer, I ride for it, and what the hell, New Orleans is at sea level and Denver is a mile above it, so you may as well hang as high as we can manage."

Paddy came back from wherever she'd been. She stared down in mingled pity and distaste, stepped over T.J.'s chained legs, and resumed her own seat by the window next to Longarm as she asked how long it was going to take them to reach Juarez. Longarm told her, "The rest of the night and change, at the rate we're going. You try and catch some shut-eye. That goes for you too, T.J. I got enough black coffee in me to see neither of you are disturbed."

T.J. sniffed and said, "I ain't sleepy. I don't want to cross the border at Juarez–El Paso, neither."

Even Paddy raised an eyebrow at that arrogant outburst. Longarm chuckled fondly and told her, "These boys never seem to grasp the simple fact that their days of wild independent thinking may be over. I recall the time I was stuck with Death Watch and this old boy they were fixing to hang in the morning said the only last meal he'd accept had to include out-of-season strawberries for dessert. He seemed to think they couldn't hang him unless and until he'd had a last meal to his liking."

Longarm glanced at T.J. to add, "He swung at sunrise, hungry. He allowed as they were leading him up the thirteen steps that he'd settle for grits and gravy after all. But by then it was too late. I don't want to hear no more about us crossing the border at Nuevo Laredo to the east, neither."

T.J. protested, "It ain't fair. I wasn't planning on having to stand trial in Colorado, durn it."

"I said that was settled," Longarm growled. "I meant it. Don't bank on me not wanting to pistol-whip you in front of a lady. Me and Miss Paddy are old pals, and your pals have made us both sort of proddy in the recent past."

T.J. started to say something else, decided not to when he read the meaning in Longarm's unwinking gray eyes, and subsided into a sullen silence.

So the overnight trip was mighty tedious for all of them, next to the train ride Longarm and Paddy had shared the last time. But all things good and bad must end, so it only felt like a million years and a hundred times that many clickety-clacks before they rolled into the Juarez yards by the dawn's early light.

Getting his prisoner, Paddy, and their baggage to the far side of the Rio Bravo was tedious as hell for Longarm, albeit more of a wake-up than the long haul by rail. A brace of Treasury Department lawmen met them on the far side of the footbridge. One took their two bags from the Mex kid Longarm had entrusted them to, so far, as the other stared soberly at the thin cotton duds the hatless prisoner had on, saying, "I see you made it tough for him to smuggle this time, Longarm. We still mean to pat him down before you take him on to Denver. For we've been told about a big jewel robbery he was mixed up in a few months back, and he's said to be a smuggling wonder as well as a thief."

Longarm nodded and said, "You left out killer. So search him all you like, as long as you don't make us miss our D and RG northbound. You can keep any nits you find on him. My outfit's only interested in nailing Murder One on him."

The revenuers thought strip-searching even T. J. Perkins in public could be put down to cruel and unusual punishment. So they promised to give the three of them a buggy ride to the depot after a short stop at the El Paso federal building. But they never made it.

That is to say, T. J. Perkins never made it there alive. For less than a city block north of the bridge a rooftop rifle squibbed and old T.J. lay sprawled on the walk in his chains while Longarm ran for a watering trough with Paddy's head and shoulders clutched under his left arm like a football.

He dove over the trough, gal and all, and left Paddy sprawled behind it, cussing, confused, but under fair cover, as he came back up, gun in hand and wary eyed.

On the far side of the street the two other federal men had broken cover with their own guns out. Nobody else was in sight, except for the facedown T.J. Both Mex and Anglo folk in such a neighborhood had sense enough to run like hell when they heard guns going off.

It only took a few minutes to determine that the

rooftop sniper had fled as well. As the survivors gathered around the remains of a man who'd already been mighty useless in life, one of the revenuers mused aloud, "That was mighty poor marksmanship if some pals was out to take him back from us."

Longarm studied on that as he stared soberly down at the dead man at his feet. The rifle round had struck dead center just below the nape of the neck. There wasn't much blood. T.J. had died instantly. Dead as anyone could get before he hit the ground.

Longarm opined, "That shot sounded like a .44-40, meaning a Wincheser, meaning a repeater, and the rest of us all seem to be alive and well after all. It's as likely they wanted him dead before he could talk."

One of the other lawmen asked about what. Longarm shrugged and said, "If I knew that, he'd have already talked. He did say something about not planning to cross here, upstream. He kept insisting he wanted to go to New Orleans by way of Nuevo Laredo. He must have had more reason than he let on. Meanwhile, we'd better put him on ice, and some embalming wouldn't hurt."

The two treasury agents exchanged glances. Then one said, "We'll be proud to have him pickled for you, once we look him over some. I take it your warrant called for delivering him to Denver dead or alive?"

Paddy gulped, tugged at Longarm's sleeve, and told him he couldn't really mean that. So Longarm assured her, "You won't have to ride all the way north to Santa Fe with him sitting up across from you. We won't be taking you home by train in the first place." Then, without answering the questions that last remark evoked from her, he told the others, "I can carry our bags as far as the Eagle Hotel. I'll rejoin you boys at the Federal Building as soon as I get this little lady out of the sun and tend to some other small chores."

So they shook on it and Longarm took Paddy to the nearby hotel he'd mentioned. The Eagle wasn't much, but he assured her they wouldn't be staying there long enough to worry about bedbugs. He explained, "I just want you out of the way, no offense, while I tidy up with the boys and hire us some good Spanish riding mules. Do you ride astride or sidesaddle, seeing you'll be doing some serious riding across the desert?"

Paddy blinked in surprise, said she rode astride on her spread, where she got to wear jeans, or sidesaddle in skirts and, of course, she wanted to know why, adding, "You can't be serious about us heading for San Miguel County on horseback!"

"Spanish mules, not horses," he said. "I know why the old-time Spaniards called the stretch from here to, say, Elephant Butte, the Journey of Death. The way we've been planning on getting you home could be deadlier. All sorts of folk may be expecting you to arrive in Santa Fe by rail, pick up the pony you left there, and head home over the Sangre de Cristo through many a handy ambush site. Trust me. I know what I'm doing."

She said she might if he kissed her good before he left her holed up in this stinky hotel. He kissed her, told her this was neither the time nor the place when she groped for his fly, and made sure she locked up after him before he went on about less pleasant but more serious business.

He lined up their mounts, saddles and provisions for at least a four-day journey, including a couple of Winchesters, before he trudged over to the Federal Building.

He had to ask about before he caught up with the naked body of his prisoner on a basement slab. They didn't get to view such a sight everyday, even in El Paso. So there were gents from the El Paso Marshal's Office as well as treasury and customs agents crowded around the wonder of the moment as Longarm joined them. One of the revenuers who'd met them nodded at Longarm to say, "He didn't even have enough dirt under his toenails to worry about. They just shot him full of corpse-pickle for you. But are you sure you want to haul him all the way to Denver? It ain't like he's about to appear before any federal judge, and we got us a swell potter's field just out on the edge of town. What would dragging him any farther prove?"

"Who he was, for certain, for one thing," Longarm said. "I wish there was a way to send photographs by wire. But there ain't. So even if I wire east for a tintype of the one and original T. J. Perkins this morning, it's still going to take 'em a few days to get here and—"

"Hold on!" a deputy from the El Paso marshal's office cut in. "Ain't this a mighty unusual time to consider who you might have just arrested on a warrant made out to Perkins and nobody else you've mentioned so far?"

Longarm got out his notebook, found the page he needed, and read off, "White male, about thirty-eight to forty, medium build, average height, black hair, blue eyes, no distinguishing scars or tattoos."

Another lawman nodded and said, "There you go. That's the way Perkins describes on the Wanted fliers they sent us."

But Longarm replied, "I wasn't reading my notes on Perkins. I took them down from the description my office sent me on one Mervin, a.k.a. Geek, Grogan. I could have sworn I left him dead in Mexico, but it just now occurred to me how ordinary both old former cellmates described. If they suckered me into bringing back the wrong man, a lot of tedious conversation about New Orleans is commencing to make a certain amount of sense!"

That set them all to buzzing. When one of them demanded to know what sense it made for one man to answer for another bound for the gallows, Longarm explained, "Hell, they'd have never hung Geek Grogan as T. J. Perkins in New Orleans. Perkins is well known as well as disliked a heap there. They expected me to deliver that old boy there, whoever he might be, and if this ain't the man they told me he was, I'd have surely wound up with egg on my face."

A revenuer said, "We'll get right on the wire for them photographs, then. We don't like to be suckered any more than you do."

But a deeper thinker sporting a deputy's badge objected, "I seem to be missing something. I can see how this dead gent might have felt reluctant to stand trial as Perkins where neither of 'em was famous. But why would their gang want to shut him up so sudden? Whether he told you along the way or waited until he had a lawyer to discuss his true identity with, it seems to me that the longer it took, the

160

more time they'd be buying for the real T. J. Perkins, if this ain't him to begin with."

Longarm nodded but said, "They've surely been moving in mysterious ways. Eating the apple a bite at a time, I want to make sure I guessed right, for a change, about this one bird we have in the hand. Both Perkins and Grogan must have posed for police photographs now and again in their travels. So it can't take more than a few days to make sure which one we have on this slab. Once I know that for certain, I'll bite off the next chaw. Meanwhile, I got a lady waiting to be escorted home. If I get her there, alive and well, I'll have eliminated some other confusion. Have any of you boys ever found yourself on two cases at once, confused as hell about just what you might be working on?"

There was a murmur of agreement. A deputy said, "In real life crooks just refuse to work neat and separate. I wish they'd cut that out."

Longarm nodded and said, "Me, too. I ought to be back in less than a week. If you boys would be kind enough to hang on to this disgusting but solid evidence for me, I might be able to deal you in on my final arrest."

They said they felt sure the body would keep that long, and naturally wanted to know what he planned on doing with it when he got back to El Paso. So Longarm said, "I'm still working on it. If I don't get back at all, feel free to bury the son of a bitch. It'll mean they were just too slick for me. It happens that way, now and again, as many a lawman could tell you, if he was still alive."

•   •   •

Longarm and Paddy O'Boyne rode north, with her astride in the new jeans he'd picked up for her. He'd taken his derringer back in exchange for the Winchester he'd bought for her. She said she knew how to use it, but didn't want to and, durn it, they seemed to be headed smack into Apache country.

He assured her the Mescalero were said to be acting calm as Mescalero ever got, and pointed out that the going was easier up the east side of the San Anres Range. It had been the desert to the *west* of said range that the early Spanish had dubbed the Journey of Death, or Jornada del Muerto, as they'd persisted in calling it.

Paddy pointed out that no Spaniard with a lick of sense had moved north through the Apache-haunted Tularosa Valley. He said that was why they were riding that way. It still failed to attract all that many travelers. So nobody would be expecting such a delicate little thing to be headed home by that route.

She showed him how delicate she felt when they camped the second night on the trail amid the mysterious white sands not even the Mescalero ever visited. There was nothing mysterious about the *location* of the white sands. The snow-white dunes extended for miles along the east side of the valley. What was mysterious was where all that pure plaster dust might have come from. The white sands weren't really sand. They were windblown gypsum, pure enough to make plaster of Paris out of. Paddy said they sure felt soft as a feather bed and took advantage of such a big private beach to scamper over the dunes as naked as she could get in the silvery moonlight. Then the cold desert air got her all goosebumped and it took him what she called a heavenly spell to warm her up again atop a blanket on a rise.

The next night they camped with weeds to spare all about. Mostly mesquite with enough cholla to make one consider where one put one's bare ass. The Tularosa Valley got more water as one worked north and, as they headed into the erosion-gone-loco maze of the Sacramento Mountains with the fairy-castle crags of El Capitan looming purple up ahead, the open patches of range between looming ridges began to be carpeted with grass. It wasn't grass as took to heavy grazing well, not growing enough to notice between rare but awesome thunderstorms. So, as they rode on, it gave way to a scalped dry stubble. Paddy proved she did know a thing or two about the cattle business when she commented on the overgrazing and asked how come, saying, "I didn't know anyone kept cows this close to Apache country."

He said, "The gent we're fixing to meet up with ain't afraid of Mescalero, or anyone else, come to study on it. If he ain't the biggest rancher between here and the Peace River he must come close. So he has more guns on his payroll than the U.S. Army has west of the Mississippi, and I suspect the Indians know that."

She gasped and asked, "Good heavens, do you mean you know Uncle John Chisum, the cattle king of New Mexico?"

"Not well enough to call him Uncle to his face. But I know he's a good old boy, as long as you don't try to cross him. I say try because, to date, nobody's ever managed to cross the one and original John Chisum entire."

"I heard about the Lincoln County War. Is it safe to assume it's over, dear?"

"Old Chisum survived it," he said. "So did one or two other mighty tough or mighty lucky gents. The shooting died down a couple of years back with the leaders of both sides wiped out. Chisum and his own gunslicks tried to steer clear of it as much as they could. That's likely why the slick old bird wound up with all the marbles when the other kids dropped out of the game."

They rode on for some mighty dry and dusty hours. Then, as the sun was painting the sky purple and gold while it got ready for bed, they rode at last into the South Springs spread of the wily old John Chisum to find him in person, rocking on the veranda of his sprawling 'dobe ranch house with a pretty young gal, dressed neater and way cleaner-faced than poor Paddy.

Old John wasn't rocking in a rocking chair. He was an independent thinker. He had one boot up against a veranda post and the straight-back chair he was seated in got to rock whether it was built for rocking or not. The veranda was shaded by the odd triple tree planted long ago out front. Longarm knew the story. Chisum was a Southern gent who'd trekked west to avoid all the bullshit brewing between the north and south. He'd planted three saplings close together in front of his new homestead in honor of his three sons, and had their tops grafted together as a reminder that kin who stuck together grew hard-to-knock-over as well as tall. The modest herd he'd started with had done some growing as well since then. John Chisum refused to say just how many head of longhorns he had his brand on these days. It was possible he was stating the simple truth when he allowed a man who could count his own infernal cows didn't have enough cows to matter.

As the tough old cattle king spied what Longarm was riding in with he rose gallantly to his feet and doffed his hat to call out, "Howdy, Longarm. Did you find that poor child lost in the desert or are you just sort of rough on women?"

Longarm helped Paddy down and proceeded to tether their saddle and pack mules as John Chisum told the other gal, "Take this poor little thing inside for a bath, a lie-down and some fresh duds, Sally. I'll find out what this lawman is up to."

He did. Longarm, knowing Chisum didn't expect men to act sissy over a little thing like a few days on the desert, took a seat on the edge of the veranda as he reached for a smoke, remembered he was out of cheroots, and said, "That lady your niece just kidnapped would be Miss Paddy O'Boyne. She claims to have a Spanish land grant up to San Miguel County. You'd know, of course."

John Chisum plunked himself back down and said, just as firmly, "She does if that's Paddy O'Boyne under all that trail dust. I knew her late father. He was all right. How come you're taking her home by way of my range? Ain't you never heard of the railroad to the west? San Miguel is a number of counties north, as I well recall with a sore behind."

Longarm wiped the sweatband of his Stetson with his kerchief as he filled the wise old cattle king in. By the time he'd finished, John Chisum had endowed him with a cigar and a light. Then he decided, "The gal's story sounds true blue. I know her tormentor, Caleb Woodward. I'll tell him he can't torment her no more. Buying a fake land grant sounds like the sort of greenhorn notion he'd fall for. I got a Mex on my payroll who likes to draw maps showing lost Spanish mines in the Sangres. He makes a little drinking money at it and it don't hurt nobody with a lick of sense."

Longarm hauled out his notebook to read off the names of the lawyers Woodward had on his own payroll. Old Chisum shrugged and said, "Them, too. Assholes from back East as ain't been out here long enough to know a royal grant from a piss ant. I don't trust any lawyer not to steal the pennies off a dead man's eyes, but nobody you've mentioned so far has ever done anything in these parts I'd really shoot him over. Like I said, I'll pass the word to my drinking pards in the Santa Fe ring and they'll see the little lady ain't pestered no more. Her dad was a good man. Until and unless she steals one of my cows we'll consider her kin and nobody *better* mess with her, hear?"

Before Longarm could reply, pretty Sally Chisum came back out with a tray of coffee and cake. As she placed it on a nail keg between Longarm and her uncle she said sweetly, "Paddy's in my tub, along with plenty of hot water and violet bath salts all the way from London Town. A girl sure does get grimy on the desert with the swimming holes so far apart."

Longarm let her pour for him as she asked her quietly if she was satisfied that was Paddy O'Boyne immersed in her salts and suds. Sally frowned sincerely to reply, "Of course that's Paddy O'Boyne. We've met before. The last time at a dance up to Las Vegas. What an odd question to ask."

Longarm took his cup from her with a sheepish

smile and said he was paid to ask dumb questions. John Chisum said, frowning pretty good himself, "You're chawing something, boy. Spit it out if you mean to spend this night under my roof. I don't hold with friends keeping secrets from one another, hear?"

Longarm smiled up at him to ask if that might include the present whereabouts of Henry McCarthy, William Bonney, or whoever Billy the Kid might really be.

John Chisum looked away and grumped, "That's different. You're a a lawman, even if you both are pals of mine. The Kid ain't been bothering nobody recently. Poor little cuss is just trying to stay alive since he busted out of the Murphy store."

Longarm said he'd heard it had been the Lincoln County Jail, to which Chisum replied with a shrug, "Same thing, now that old Major Murphy don't own nothing in these parts no more." He took a bite of his cake, washed it down, and mused soberly, "I tried to tell both sides they were acting dumb. Had I thought war made any sense it might have been me instead of Robert E. Lee who led the boys in butternut against the north. I'd have likely won, too. But, like I said, there's just no sense in fighting a war when you don't have to. They should have listened. There was enough to go around out here. But some gents seem to be just natural hogs as can't abide other hogs at the same trough. Billy was all right. He was just young and foolish."

Sally Chisum confided, "I danced with him one night, right out back on the patio. Do you remember, Uncle John?"

"I do," John Chisum grumbled. "He asked before I could tell you he was Billy the Kid. I told him not to do that no more and he never, as I also recalls."

She said, sort of dreamy eyed, "He was ever so polite and shy. A good dancer, too. I still can't believe he killed all those men some say he has."

"I don't buy that many either," Longarm said. Then he turned back to her uncle to say, "I know you don't want to talk about the Kid with me, and I respect your reasons. But could you tell me about the so-called Regulators he was riding with, earlier in the Lincoln County War?"

Big John shrugged and said, "That was just a fool notion as didn't work worth beans. Seeing the Murphy faction had the local sheriff bought off, Lawyer McSween thought he could deputize his own boys to go after cattle thieves the sheriff didn't seem to notice. The crooks we had up to Santa Fe before Lew Wallace was appointed to clean things up said sticking a tin badge on a hired gun was unlawful. They were likely right. Takes a crook to know a crook. Billy wasn't pretending to be a deputy when he gunned Sheriff Brady in the back. He done it as a public service. By then the so-called Regulators had all tossed away their fool badges and joined one side or the other as plain old hired guns. I hate it when men change sides like that. They do that a lot in wars. That's why I try to stay outta 'em."

Longarm nodded soberly and said, "The war I run off to join as a kid turned out unpleasant too. My point is that all the old New Mexico Regulators have been killed, gone straight, or leastways scattered?"

John Chisum nodded and said, "They have. Are you saying you suspect that dude Woodward of sending *Regulators* after that sweet child inside? You're barking up the wrong tree, boy. I told you Woodward was just dumb. He ain't got no connections like that in these parts. It's got hard to hire a New Mexico gun who don't know you all the way back to your grandparents. Lots of kids got betrayed in the recent dustup and only the smart ones survived."

Longarm asked about hiring no-goods in other parts and mentioned the oily Gomez over by Nuevo Laredo. The older man shrugged and said, "Any gringo lawyer wanting to do business in Old Mexico would have to get in touch with a Mex lawyer, even Woodward's. I don't doubt your Gomez is a crook. They don't have no other kind of gent practicing law under El Presidente Diaz. But I can't say I know anything more than that about a border-town hack by any Mex handle. I try to avoid business dealings down that way. I get cheated enough by the rascals back East."

Longarm put down his empty cup, rose, stretched, and told them both how neighborly he considered them. As he moved away from the veranda Chisum demanded, "What are you up to now? It's almost dark, and don't you want a bath as soon as that young gal gets out of the tub?"

Longarm shook his head and said, "It ain't as if I'll ever forget Miss Paddy O'Boyne, but I see I can forget about her as far as the case I'm working on goes. You've convinced me all the worry I went through on her behalf was a pure red herring, and it's time I got back on the true trail."

Sally protested, "Don't you even mean to say adios to the poor girl? She told me, just now, that she sort of likes you."

Longarm smiled wistfully and said, "I like her too. But now that I see she's safe in good strong

169

hands, I have to ride for El Paso again, sudden. For this puzzle is commencing to fit together more sensible, now that I've got rid of all the pieces I just couldn't get to fit together!"

They'd have surely wanted to know more, had he stuck around to jaw with them. But he'd wasted more time than he could spare on what he now saw as a fool's errand.

But a few hot and dusty days later, as he was riding back across the now even emptier looking white sands, he had to allow all the time he'd wasted on a gal who'd never been in all that much trouble to begin with hadn't been *totally* wasted.

Chapter 11

The photographs they'd wired east for had beaten Longarm to El Paso easy. As he viewed them in an upstairs office with the treasury men who'd already been disgusted by them, Longarm nodded and said, "It's like I feared. The one I hope you still have on ice for me was a ringer. They knew the border was being watched tighter than usual by you boys. You didn't need photographs to suspect a blue-eyed gent of Perkins's general description might not be a Mexican fruit picker on his way to work on our side of the border. So they bribed some corrupt rurales, as if there was any other kind, to sucker the Justice Department to send a fool like me to Nuevo Laredo to pick him up. It was all an act. I was diddled into chasing Geek Grogan all over Mexico with the distinct impression he was the real T. J. Perkins."

One of the revenuers said, "But didn't you tell us you thought you might have gunned the real thing down Mexico way?"

Longarm nodded and said, "It wasn't supposed to work out that way. I was supposed to bring back the one I brung back. Once you boys heard a U.S. deputy had captured Perkins, how close might you have been watching for him along the border?"

The other lawmen exchanged glances. One said, "In that case it was dumb as hell of them to shoot their ringer in front of all of us. Had you just gone on to Denver with him it might have took weeks for any one of us to tumble to the sneaky trick. They surely paid the fake Perkins enough to keep him quiet a spell. He'd have had no reason to rat on himself before they were set to hang him, right?"

Longarm shrugged and said, "Well, he never told me he was the wrong man, not wanted federal, even when I put leg irons on him."

The other revenuer frowned and said, "They must have feared he'd tell you something worse, then. It couldn't have been that the real Perkins was dead. Who would have cared?"

Before Longarm could reply the older of the two revenuers shot his junior sidekick a disgusted look and said, "The mastermind behind all this bullshit, of course. Ain't it obvious by now that a heap of planning must have gone into all this razzle-dazzle? If Grogan knew his pal, Perkins, wasn't ever going to smuggle beans, he might have talked to save himself the bother of riding all the way to Denver in chains for nothing."

The younger revenuer insisted, "It was still dumb to murder him right in front of us all. Don't you think so, Longarm?"

Longarm shrugged and said, "They likely figured he was no further use to them a railroad stop north. Why don't we just bury the poor bastard, print it in the papers that we're doing so, and see who shows up?"

The older revenuer laughed incredulously and asked, "You mean, for his funeral? An outlaw would have to be dumb as hell before he'd come to the funeral of a sidekick being planted by the U.S. government, wouldn't he? I thought you said the rascals had been acting mighty slick up to now."

Longarm nodded and said, "Slick and ruthless. We can make the afternoon editions with his obit if we box him for potter's field right now. I'd be obliged if you boys could handle that chore for me. I'd like a bath and a shave after all the time I just spent riding in circles, if it's all the same to you."

The senior revenuer assured Longarm he knew how to bury a skunk, since he'd done so before. So they shook on it and Longarm agreed to meet them out by potter's field no later than seven-thirty. The one who'd agreed to plant the cuss frowned and asked, "As late as that, Longarm? The sun will be fixing to sink shortly after, you know."

Longarm nodded and said, "It's got to set total before we'll see any real action. You wasn't expecting his pals to show up in broad daylight, were you?"

It was actually closer to ten and the old burial ground was downright dark and spooky by the time the younger of the two revenuers with two El Paso deputies hunkered in the mesquite with Longarm and decided, "It's late enough. The bats have even quit flying, and if anyone else was coming they'd have been here by now."

Longarm was pleased to see he didn't have to be the one to hush the fool kid. Another lawman staked out with him growled, "Run home to your momma, then. Anyone can see you've never staked out a grave marker or anything else before!"

The restless youth subsided. It got later. Longarm knew most cat burglars liked to work around four in the morning. He saw no reason to mention that. He hadn't expected it to be a short night. He knew the boredom would get worse long before it was apt to get better.

Then someone hissed, "Someone's coming!"

And sure enough they heard someone trip over a wooden marker to wail, in a mighty female voice for an outlaw, "Yoo-hoo, Custis? Custis Long? I know you're around here someplace, you sneaky brute!"

That voice just couldn't belong to the pest he feared it might. But it did, once he'd hissed Miss Sparky Whatever from the *Omaha Herald* into the brush along the edge of the graveyard. The perky little reporter gal had gotten him in a heap of needless trouble the time they'd met at the Great State Fair up Nebraska way. He warned her, "Miss Sparky, this time I really mean it. If you get in my line of fire I'll shoot through you with a clear conscience, knowing you had it coming. Who told you what was up out here, you nosy little thing?"

She stared up at him with her big baby-blue eyes, knowing the effect that had on men who liked blondes with perky breasts, and answered, "Nobody told me what was up. All I needed to know was that you'd had a hand in planting a famous outlaw out this way, you sneak. I've never forgiven you for the time you snuck out on me right after—" Then she clammed up with a blush as she became aware of the other lawmen grinning at them.

Longarm introduced her all around as Omaha's answer to Nelly Bligh and told her, "All right, as long as you're here I don't want you tripping over no more grave markers with your dainty high-buttons. But for God's sake keep your pretty head down, and that goes for your pretty behind as well."

174

She hunkered down in the mesquite, but kept asking him what the story was, adding she'd do most anything for a scoop.

He said, "We already established that in Omaha. I ain't sure what the full story is, yet. If my hunch is right, you'll beat all the other papers to press with it. If I'm wrong, well, I'm sort of glad to meet up with you again, Sparky."

She told him not to get any ideas. She was always saying dumb things like that. He told her to just hush. It was tedious enough out here without having to worry about an erection. He tried not to think about that time they'd met in Omaha. It was so hard to forget that it served to pass more time. Then someone else out there tripped over a grave marker and Longarm was all ears, and all eyes, as they all saw the bull's-eye lantern coming their way, swinging its narrow beam about. When the cuss holding it got to the wooden plank with T. J. Perkins written on it he stopped to call softly, *"Aqui! Pronto, pero silencio!"* So four gents packing picks, guns and shovels joined him fast and sneaky as he'd told 'em to. Two of them got right down to digging as the others stood watch. Anyone could see how proddy they were. Anyone but Sparky. She gasped, "Oh, why are they robbing that grave?" And though she hadn't whispered all that loud, they'd heard her. So the next few seconds got noisy as hell.

Longarm flattened Sparky in the dust with one hand as he fired at the one with the lantern with the other. That kept the other side from sweeping the mesquite with more than gunfire as everyone but the pesky blonde threw lead at one another. But the late-night visitors were in the open, Longarm and his pals were firing from cover, and so it was all over soon enough.

Longarm moved in ahead of his survivors to pick up the still-burning bull's-eye and shine it down at the strangers sprawled in the graveyard dirt all about. When he shone the beam on a face he'd seen before, he called out, "This one's Gomez, the border-town lawyer I told you boys about. Since the others look Anglo and he saw fit to boss them about in his own lingo, I'd say he must have been the boss. The boss of this bunch, at any rate. We ain't allowed to arrest Diaz, neither, and I doubt any Mex members of the combine will be paying us a visit, now that we've settled this disgusting business."

Sparky plucked at his sleeve to ask him what he was talking about. He said, "I told you to stay put. If you'd kept your pretty trap shut we'd have gotten these cusses to dig the body up for us before we had to arrest 'em."

One of the other lawmen opined, "I doubt they'd have come quiet. I never seen such proddy cusses robbing graves before. What do you reckon they was after, Longarm? We buried their pal in nothing but an old sheet, as I recall."

"They weren't after his worthless carcass," Longarm said. "They were after what they hoped to find inside it. Grogan was a circus freak as could swallow most anything he put his mind to. Now we got to dig him up and see what he smuggled across the border, under guard, in his damned old stomach."

Chapter 12

Longarm got back to Denver late of an afternoon to
find that his boss, Marshal Vail, was off down the
hall of the Federal Building on other business. So
being no fool, Longarm handed the clerk the notes
he'd written up aboard the train and got out of there
pronto to see if a certain widow woman up to Sher-
man Avenue still liked him.

She did. So he showed up sort of late for work the
next morning. But that wasn't what seemed to be
bothering Billy Vail the most. He barely glanced at
the banjo clock on his oak-paneled wall as he sat
Longarm down across the desk from him and
growled, "I have been informed by the Treasury Department that they are mighty pleased with you. And
Mexico hasn't bitched about you this time, so you
must have done *something* right."

Then he waved the report Henry had typed up, to
growl even worse, "I just wish I knew what in
thunder you'd done! I know you always leave the
dirty parts out and don't like to repeat yourself, but I
can't make heads or tails out of this terse account of
complicated diamond smuggling, save the fact it
reads mighty disgusting in places."

Longarm leaned back in the leather guest chair to
haul out a smoke as he explained, "The motives were
simple enough, boss. It was the execution of the

basic plot as got so wheels-within-wheels to even rascals on the other side."

He lit his cheroot, shook out the match, and after gazing about in vain for an ashtray, tucked it in his hat brim.

Then he said, "In the beginning there was T. J. Perkins with some hot diamonds of the first water to smuggle across the border. He'd done that once too often in the past and knew his face was famous. There were plenty of other crooks who didn't look at all like him. But there ain't really that much honor among thieves. So he figured he could only entrust his goodies to someone who'd have a tough time just running off with 'em once they'd made it back to the land of opportunity. That was where the late Geek Grogan came in. Aside from Grogan's being a freak who could swallow most anything and vomit it at will, Perkins also recalled him from their time in prison together as a gent who answered to his own description and could pass for him to the casual eye."

Vail shook his bullet head and said, "That's the part I just don't get. Why in thunder would a famous smuggler want a man who could be taken for him smuggling doodly-shit? Couldn't he see such a gent would surely be searched with enthusiasm at any border crossing?"

Longarm flicked ash on the rug to preserve it from carpet mites, ignored the dirty look Vail shot at him, and said, "That was the main point Perkins had in mind. A sweet old lady or just anyone slipping across the border undetected where the river's shallow would be free to double-cross Perkins. He didn't want to be double-crossed. He wanted his diamonds to come into this country under armed guard. I was the sucker he chose for that chore, as it turned out. Any lawman who had Geek Grogan in leg irons and didn't know he was stuffed with stolen jewelry might have done as well. The plan was for Grogan to pack the diamonds across the border in a way that left him little freedom of movement. He was told he had to follow the plan to the letter if he didn't want to wind up hanging for murder in place of Perkins. I was supposed to deliver him to the federal lockup at New Orleans. Once there, he was to privately puke up a rubber contraceptive full of jewelry and hand it over to the right confederate. The customs boys are working on just who that might have been. They ought to ferret him out easy enough."

Vail said, "I know some guards feel they ain't paid near enough, and watch where you flick them damned ashes. Are you trying to tell me a man can wander about for days or more with a bellyful of diamonds? What's to stop nature from taking her course? How could even a circus freak keep from shitting jewels all the way to New Orleans?"

"The rubber they were in," Longarm said. "A lump that size can't pass through the lower valve of your stomach. So it don't. The diamonds were there to stay until Geek Grogan felt like puking them up. Once he did, in New Orleans, another crooked lawyer like Gomez would have him out of jail in no time. It was a pure fact that the man I was supposed to deliver like a fool just wasn't the man as shot them customs agents. So any fool lawyer could prove that by the time his case came to trial."

Vail brightened and said, "I get it. Had he tried to keep the goodies for himself, it would have been just

179

as easy to let him swing in the place of Perkins, right?"

Longarm shrugged and observed, "Almost as easy. They must have known all along that Grogan had a fair chance of proving he was another man if he really had to. They were hoping the poor petty crook was too dumb or nervous to risk that. When they saw he wasn't headed for New Orleans after all, they figured he *was*, and jumped to conclusions unfortunate as hell for him. But I see I'm getting ahead of my story."

"Then stick to the story and watch them damned ashes!" Vail said.

So Longarm continued, "The basic plan was simple, as I just said. But they had to sucker some lawman to carry Grogan and guard their diamonds as far as New Orleans. They had that crook, Gomez, hire some crooked rurales to wire us that Perkins had been picked up and was ready to be extradited. They had no way of knowing our Denver office had a prior claim on him. The rest you know."

Vail snapped, "That'll be the day! Why in thunder did you go all the way to Mexico City to clap irons on the fake Perkins if he was on ice for you in Nuevo Laredo? Why couldn't you have just frog-marched him back across the bridge?"

Longarm took a drag on his cheroot, shrugged, and said, "Honor among thieves. There ain't that much. Perkins wasn't about to let the rubberful of diamonds out of his sight before he saw I'd taken the bait. He had every reason to feel uneasy as close to the border as Nuevo Laredo. So they must have argued about it some before Gomez saw a brass ring and grabbed it for the gang."

Longarm started to flick more ash on the rug, decided he'd best catch 'em in his hat, and explained, "An otherwise innocent land-hog called Woodward had been sold a fake Spanish land grant. Gents with time on their hands whip out treasure maps as often, for drinking money. Woodward was green enough to go for it. He challenged the proper owner of considerable range on the authenticity of her real land grant. Gomez was one of the legal hacks who got word of the nonsense as the usual blizzard of claims and counterclaims commenced. When he learned Miss Paddy O'Boyne was bound for Old Mexico he had confederates scare her into crossing the border at Nuevo Laredo. He had to work there because you don't find even a crooked rurale captain just any old place, and he figured any lawman wanting to carry Perkins to New Orleans would find Nuevo Laredo handy. They tucked Grogan, as Perkins, in the rurale lockup just before I arrived, arrested me when I showed up for him, and arranged the charade whereby I'd wind up recapturing the fake Perkins just after he'd inhaled the only objects of real interest to the bastards. They didn't care one way or the other about ladies or land grants. So I left out some of the fun I had down Mexico way as unimportant, and I'm sorry if I confused you, boss."

Vail sighed and said, "I just told you I didn't care about the disgusting way you carry on around poor innocent women. You were suckered into arresting Grogan as Perkins in Ciudad Mejico. Get to the shoot-out in El Paso."

"I shot the real Perkins earlier," Longarm said, "thinking he was Geek Grogan. But since that wasn't in our jurisdiction, let's get to El Paso like you said. I wasn't supposed to take either of the rascals to El Paso. Things just worked out that way because I'm so noble. With Perkins dead and Geek Grogan suddenly headed the wrong way, the rest of the gang didn't know what in hell was up. So they laid Grogan low to keep him from going anywhere."

Vail asked, "What good did that do them? Was it revenge for a double-cross they suspected?"

Longarm shook his head and said, "They didn't care about poor Grogan. All they knew was that he was stuffed with something they valued more. They must have expected us to bury him right off, and since the El Paso potter's field is on this side of the border—"

"Oh my God!" Vail cut in. "Are you saying they meant to dig him up and gut him like a chicken for the pebbles in his craw?"

Longarm nodded soberly and said, "They must have. They were digging up his grave when me and the treasury boys closed in on 'em. It was U.S. Customs as opened him up in the end. I had no call to, once I seen I'd got my man, with one left over. They seemed mighty pleased with the results of the autopsy. If you ask me, half a million dollars wasn't near enough to pay for the trouble all of us was put through. And speaking of money, old Henry, out front, just told me there's sure to be a fuss from the accounting office over some of the modest expenses I was forced to charge to my traveling allowance."

Vail smiled thinly and said, "Now *that* part of your report affords me no mystery at all. What do you mean by asking the government to spring for a honeymoon suite in El Paso, after you'd carried that

O'Boyne gal to safety and come back to finish off the Perkins gang?"

Longarm smiled sheepishly and said, "I couldn't catch me a train out until I'd done some paperwork for the El Paso coroner and, well, you wouldn't have wanted me sleeping like a bum in the railroad depot them few nights, would you?"

Vail marveled, "Double occupancy with an adjoining bath, and the coroner's office closed for the Sabbath as well? You sure got balls, old son."

Longarm smiled modestly to reply, "So I was just told, down El Paso way." Billy Vail just had to laugh like hell despite himself. So, in the end, they split the difference.

Watch for

LONGARM AND THE REBEL KILLERS

one hundred twenty-ninth novel in the bold
LONGARM series
from Jove

coming in September!

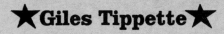
204

203